Soul of a Monster 3

Lock Down Publications and
Ca$h Presents
Soul of a Monster 3
A Novel by **Aryanna**

Lock Down Publications
P.O. Box 870494
Mesquite, Tx 75187

Visit our website
www.lockdownpublications.com

First Edition April 2020
Printed in the United States of America

This is a work of fiction. Names, characters, places, and incidents either are products of the author's imagination or are used fictitiously. Any similarity to actual events or locales or persons, living or dead, is entirely coincidental.

Lock Down Publications
Like our page on Facebook: Lock Down Publications @
www.facebook.com/lockdownpublications.ldp
Cover design and layout by: **Dynasty Cover Me**
Book interior design by: **Shawn Walker**
Edited by: **Kiera Northington**

Stay Connected with Us!

Text **LOCKDOWN** to 22828 to stay up-to-date
with new releases, sneak peeks, contests and more…

Submission Guideline.

Submit the first three chapters of your completed manuscript to ldpsubmissions@gmail.com, subject line: Your book's title. The manuscript must be in a .doc file and sent as an attachment. The document should be in Times New Roman, double-spaced and in size 12 font. Also, provide your synopsis and full contact information. If sending multiple submissions, they must each be in a separate email.

Have a story but no way to send it electronically? You can still submit to LDP/Ca$h Presents. Send in the first three chapters, written or typed, of your completed manuscript to:

LDP: Submissions Dept
Po Box 870494
Mesquite, Tx 75187

DO NOT send original manuscript. Must be a duplicate.

Provide your synopsis and a cover letter containing your full contact information.

Thanks for considering LDP and Ca$h Presents.

Dedication:

This book is dedicated to McKenzie because I love you still.

Acknowledgements:

First and foremost I give all glory to God for all the blessings that he continues to give me. I'm not sure that I deserve all that I've been given but I'll continue to be humble and appreciative. I have to thank my significant other because you've put up with SO MUCH SHIT when it comes to me! I don't know how you don't leave, or why, but I hope one day to be worthy of your love. Love doesn't owe a debt, but I OWE you! I have to thank my twin, Aryanna, for loving me the way that only you can. I won't give you a bunch of pretty words sweetheart, I'll give you my life instead. I love you Little F!!! I have to thank Connor (the owner of dumb dumb), and Natalie (the shit starter) because I love you both, and you love me back. I'll see you soon. I have to thank all of my family that supports me. The love is real, I have to thank all of my fans, old and new, because I can't do this without you. I have to thank my haters for continuing to fuel the fire in my stomach. I'm hungrier than ever!!! I have to thank those who take care of me on a daily basis; Kayla (both of you crazy females), the crazy island girl, Boss Queen Ross, the big bad bear, Mo-Mo (a place in Alabama), the Grinch, Brittany (the appointment), and DT (the Baltimore's biggest fan). You all put up with my bullshit, and I appreciate it. I have to thank Sgt. Lightskin (pigeon toed asshole). I remind you of your brother, so I know you love me and I love you too. I'll see you under different lights. I have to thank too short (red dread bandit) for reminding me of my station in life. I know where I need to be, and I'm on the way.

Now for the roll call...SHOUT OUT TO: Rex (My favorite cousin), Meat Rock (My shadow), Big Bam (last of a dying breed), Jeezy, Red, B. Havoc, Silk, Dub, Duke (ace for the real niggas), Bird, J (the Baltimore legend), the whole dmv behind the g-wall, Ashley (too tall), Polo (hype program founder), Pree (little big bruh), and all the real niggas I've met along the way. Keep your head up because if it ain't life it ain't long.

I have to thank Cash and my whole LDP family. We ride together, we die together. PERIOD! If there's anyone I forgot I'm sorry, but I thank you in spirit. I love everyone who loves me...and if you don't love me that's ok too because I love your hate! THE GAME IS OURS!!!!

Chapter 1
September 2021
Amsterdam
Honey

"It's me."

"Are you sure you're ready for this?" Aubrey asked. Despite this being something like the millionth time she'd asked me this question, it always took my mind back to the night not so long ago, when I'd killed a fifteen-year-old girl by accident. I'd never known guilt like the one that came from dropping the hammer on an innocent child and snuffing out their life, and I knew that I'd never be the same after that moment. At the time, I thought that would be the one kill that haunted me the most, but it wasn't. Killing the love of my life was. Putting two bullets in Dollar had taken something from me, something I could only identify as the last of humanity's hold on my soul. When Dollar died, he took my soul with him, so now killing was the only way I knew to soothe what was constantly restless inside. Killing was my ticket to finding peace.

"The bills gotta get paid, sis," I replied.

"Don't give me that lame shit, because you know money ain't never gonna be an issue for you. Granted, I don't know where Dollar stashed *all* his money, but the account he'd designated for you has more money in it then you could spend in twenty lifetimes of the rich and famous."

I knew she was telling the truth, but she didn't understand that I couldn't spend a dime of that money. If she'd known how Dollar actually died, she wouldn't have offered me shit except a well-placed bullet, but that secret was mine to keep under lock and key. Along with the guilt. For months, I felt justified in killing my husband and sister for their whorish ways of fucking each other behind my back. I slept good every night, knowing they were burning in the hottest pits of hell for what they'd done to me. All that changed with the birth of my son though. From the time the doctor laid him on my chest and I stared into his dark brown eyes, all I could see was the man I loved more than anything staring back at me. I'd thought I'd prepared myself the whole time I was pregnant for the very real possibility my son could look like his father, but when I saw him I knew I could've never truly prepared. Tears of joy became tears of sadness, and the first brick of guilt was laid upon my heart. Two months later, I felt crushed beneath that guilt, and that's part of what had driven me from the safety of my hiding spot to the dingy motel room I now sat in, waiting on a kill order. I was smart enough to know that I was trying to outrun the impossible, but I didn't care. Right now, I just didn't care.

"I need to do this, Aubrey. I need to release all that's been bottled up for the last ten months since-since..."

"I get it, sis. I miss him too, and that's part of the reason I'm so worried about you right now. I feel like Dollar would *still* find some way to kill me if I let something happen to you. He loved you more than life and everything in it."

"I like to think he did," I said softly.

"Oh, there's *no doubt* he did. My brother was a flawed man, and he did unspeakable things, but he absolutely loved you. You were his Honey."

I could taste the salty tears pouring into my mouth at the bittersweet memories playing in my mind. It was unreal how my body still tingled at the thought of my first sexual encounter with Dollar. He'd nicknamed me Honey before that, but once he saw my eyes change colors after I reached orgasm, he'd known how perfectly suited that name was. Thinking about that night and the next morning, how we went from fucking to making love, only made me miss him more right now. And it made my pussy throb with want. Part of me had wanted to go out and fuck a nigga on more than one occasion while I was pregnant, and I would've been justified, but I couldn't do it. Something inside me refused to let another man lay one finger on me, so in a lust-filled moment I'd done the unthinkable and got a tattoo on my pussy. It said: Property of Dollar.

"I loved him, Aubrey. I swear to God, I did. I still do."

"I know that, Honey, and no matter where he is, I'm sure he knows that too."

It was on the tip of my tongue to tell her why that last part of her statement might not be accurate, but I chose to refocus my energy instead.

"Doing this makes me feel closer to him, Aubrey, and I know you can understand that better than anyone else."

My words brought only silence over the line, but a few moments later, the laptop in front of me alerted me to a new encrypted file I'd just received.

"Thanks, sis," I said.

"Just be safe. I don't mind babysitting Kyla and Dorian, but they need you to be their mother."

"I know that. I'll be home in a few days," I replied, disconnecting our call quickly. I knew I was being rude, but I didn't wanna take the chance that she'd put one of the kids on the phone. My little man couldn't do more than coo into the phone, but Kyla could and would ask questions. The one thing she always wanted to know was when her daddy was coming back. Dorian looked so much like his dad that poor Kyla was afraid to let him out of her sight, because she didn't wanna lose him too. She woke up looking for her brother and went to sleep crying for her daddy. It broke my heart, and added yet another brick of guilt to my growing collection.

"Get it together, girl," I said aloud, shaking my head to clear my thoughts. My mind needed to be completely focused on the target. Jeffery Sentiles was a successful businessman from the United States that liked to use Europe as his playground. His private jet was due to touch down in Amsterdam in just over sixteen hours, and he would be here long enough to make good use of the RedLight District. I had seventy-two hours to plan and carry out Mr. Sentiles's execution, so I blocked every-thing from my mind and focused on the job at hand. The dossier Aubrey sent was as detailed as always, listing everything about Jeffery down to which hand he wiped his ass with. Like most old, rich, white men, Jeff was "exocentric" when it came to his bedroom activities, which really translated into him being weird as fuck. Seduction was the easiest tool for a woman to use when it came to disarming a man, because it was virtually impos-sible for them to think with both heads at the same time. Even with me knowing that, it still didn't stop my stom-ach from rolling at the thought of what I might have to do while in character of seductress. The client who was paying for the job didn't want it to look like an overnight hit, and that meant I had to give serious consideration to playing the whore Jeffery desired. I laid down across the single bed taking up half of the tiny motel room, and began to study the file on my laptop intensely. When the makings of a few acceptable plans took root in my brain, I sent Aubrey a message with a list of the shit I needed. With that done, I decided to give my tired eyes a needed break while smoking one of the blunts provided by the motel. The room I was in was a low budget knock-off to Motel 6 or Super 8 back in the U.S., but the weed they provided was *fire*. I managed to get a little more than halfway through the blunt, before I had to put it out and lay down. Despite me being high as shit, I still couldn't outrun the ever present nightmares that tormented me. The dream was *always* the same. In it I'd emptied my clip into Dollar, but instead of dying, he stood up and told me he loved me. I don't know what my subconscious was trying to tell me, but the ache in my chest always followed me back to my conscious moments. So did the tears. When I finally awoke the next morning, I could feel that my eyes were swollen and puffy from crying in my sleep, making me thankful I was waking up alone instead of next to the kids. I dragged myself out of bed, and managed to find my way to the shower without turning on any lights or opening the blinds. Once I was beneath the pounding spray of the hot water, I waited for the next phase of my morning ritual to begin. I tried to clear my mind in hopes that if I thought about absolutely nothing then I wouldn't feel shit either, but of course that didn't work. The tears still came like they always did, starting out slow at first and eventually building in intensity, until I could barely breathe. No matter what anger I felt towards Dollar or what justification I used for killing him, I still mourned every single day I woke up without him by my side. The love I felt for him was just as strong as the

Aryanna

first day I'd understood that we were supposed to be together forever. I knew my love would last even though forever was never as long as it seemed. Once I was able to pull myself together, I quickly bathed myself, and then I completed my morning ritual by rubbing my clit until my pussy spasmed violently from my climax. Making my pussy squirt was my tribute to Dollar because there had never been a man who made me feel all that he did, especially when it came to sex. On wobbly knees, I stepped out of the shower, dried off and got dressed. When I checked my encrypted email, I received the location for the safehouse where my requested materials were stashed, and that meant that the hunt was on. After packing my small overnight bag, and wiping all traces of my presence from the room and shower, I called for a Lyft to take me to my destination. Half an hour later, I was standing in an apartment that was fully furnished to look like someone's grandmother lived there. The grenade launcher, AR-25, ammunition, and necessary accessories that were spread out on the living room floor where the only things that were completely out of place in this environment. I put some black latex gloves on, did a quick check to make sure that everything I needed was there, and once I was satisfied, I shot Aubrey a text from my burner phone. I grabbed a Glock .27 and an extra clip, tucking the clip in my pocket while securing the pistol at the small of my back in the waist of my cargo pants. After throwing on a black flight jacket, I grabbed the helmet and key off the table, and headed for the bike out front. It was time to do a little sightseeing and the all black Honda CBR 1000 would allow me to do that at whatever pace I felt comfortable. My bulky clothing and the fact that my short hair was covered by the helmet made it impossible

14

to identify my five foot four, one-hundred-sixty-pound-frame as male or female, and that's just how I wanted it. I got on the move and did my tourist thing for a little over two hours, before returning to the safe house with a plan in mind. I spent the better part of the day looking at Geo maps, creating several different escape routes from the location I would strike at. Once I was sure I had a way out no matter what, I had Aubrey hack into the police database to find and compare the response times when the authorities were called. Studying that allowed me to give myself the necessary window to accomplish my goal, and with that done the clock began ticking towards Jeffery's ending. I waited until dusk before I was back on my bike, with a backpack under my flight jacket, concealing all the materials I needed. Once I arrived across the street from the whore house, I knew Jeffery would start with, I swiftly assembled the AR-25 and fitted it with an extended thirty-round magazine. I laid the loaded grenade launcher beside it, and waited as the shadows closed in on the alley I was hiding in. An hour later, it was so dark that I could barely see my hand in front of my face, which meant nobody looking in my direction would be able to spot me. Exactly twenty-eight minutes after that, a gray Rolls Royce eased to the curb across the street from me, and within moments Jeffery was escorted from the backseat into the whorehouse. I was a little surprised that he wasn't wearing some type of disguise, but then again, sex sold legally in this country so there was no shame in it. I waited patiently for fifteen more minutes, and then I set the timer on my watch that said I had three minutes to become one with the wind. I took a deep breath, lifted the grenade launcher, and fired two shots through the parlor windows. Surprised screams could be heard seconds before simultaneous explosions rocked the ground beneath my feet. Chunks of concrete rained from the sky as the fire quickly spread from the row of houses to the cars out front up and down the sidewalk. That triggered more explosions as twisted metal screamed into the night sky, but my focus was now on the people running out of the whorehouses. I put my eye to the scope of the AR-25, took a deep breath, and slowly exhaled as I squeezed the trigger. I chose targets at random, shooting both males and females with the ease and expertise of a video gamer. To me, this wasn't as fun as video games, but it was necessary because this whole thing would go down as a terror attack instead of hit. The moment I spotted Jeffery trying to run for his life, I double tapped the trigger, and forever separated his left and right brain. Once he dropped, I quickly switched guns again and fired two more grenades for good measure. This time when the ground shook I felt it beneath the motorcycle tires, but it didn't stop me from speeding away. I could still hear the screams as I vanished, but they didn't move me one way or another. This was just a job, and the part of me that cared about life and death ceased to exist a long time ago. I was reborn now, and I was ok with that. In fact, it's what I wanted.

Chapter 2
Louisiana

"I-I can't b-breathe."

"Shut the fuck up then," I growled, my grip on her throat tightened steadily as I pushed my dick inside her faster and harder. Even as her face turned a deeper shade of red, I could tell the way her eyes rolled were a result of pleasures, not panic. With every stroke, it seemed like her pussy got wetter, and her grip tightened as mine did. The heat of our flesh fought with the humidity in the air for dominance, but somehow our combined sweat made our coupling sexier to me.

"D-D-Dollar!" she panted, clawing at my back until my skin came away under her nails.

I didn't need her to verbally tell me what was happening because I could feel that last door opening as my dick beat on her walls without mercy. I finally released my grip on her neck, and grabbed her right leg for leverage while I pounded her into orgasmic bliss. The feeling of her pussy gushing all over me made me cum with the force of a broken fire hydrant, but I didn't stop my onslaught of strokes until both of us lay here too weak for words. I tried to roll out of her, but she kept her other leg wrapped around me so that she ended up on top of me, with my dick still very much inside her.

"You're gonna make me hurt you," I warned.

"You ain't did it yet, at l-least not in a way I can't handle."

Her smile was full of bad intentions, but I wasn't paying attention to her for real. I closed my eyes so she wouldn't see my mind wander, because if she saw that then she'd undoubtedly know who I was thinking about. I tried to control when my mind drifted off into this danger zone, but sometimes it was beyond my control. My hand went to the two bullet holes in my chest that were only three inches apart, and a half an inch away from my heart. I rubbed the scar tissue softly while asking myself the same question I had asked for the last ten months. Did she miss my heart on purpose, or was it luck?

"Does your chest hurt?"

"No, I'm fine," I replied, letting my hand drop to my side.

The feeling of her lips kissing my scars only made my emotions more conflicted, but I didn't push her away because I knew it would hurt her feelings. Instead, I let her kiss on me, and kept my eyes closed so I could see Honey in my mind. When I felt her sliding down my body and taking my dick in her mouth, I envisioned it was my sweet Honey deep throating me. I gave myself over to the moment, wrapping my left hand up in her hair and letting her suck me nice and slowly. My mind went back to the first time Honey ever devoured me. The look of determination and hunger is her golden colored eyes as they blazed up at me through the darkness made me feel like her prey, and I had loved it. She hadn't simply been sucking my dick, she'd been pulling my soul from my body. I hadn't known it then, but even if I had, I still would've given in to her because the love between us was destined to be. How the fuck had it all gone wrong? Did I really deserve the punishment she'd handed out? These questions rattle around my brain for months, but I had no answer and that made me angry.

"Why did you stop?" I asked, opening my eyes and looking down.

It took me a minute to understand the fear and confusion in Katie's eyes, but when I realized I had her hair in my left hand and my gun aimed at her head with my right I understood. I quickly lowered the gun and pushed it under the pillow, but it still took a few moments for her expression to return to normal.

"Do-do you want me to finish?"

"No, it's okay," I replied, pulling her towards me and holding her.

"I'm sorry, Katie. I just—"

"You don't have to explain, I know what happened," she said softly.

Her words held no judgement, and I appreciated that more than I did the blow job. The pain of almost dying at the hands of someone you once trusted was a pain Katie could understand and identify with, for more than one reason. That made words unnecessary for the moment, so we simply laid there and took comfort from the mutual silence. If somebody would've told me a year ago that I'd be in this situation with this *woman* of all people providing me with comfort I would've laughed, and then shot the muthafucka who said it. Even if I had known that Katie had survived my attempt to kill her all those years ago when she betrayed me, I still wouldn't have imagined we'd end up between sweaty sheets again. Then again, I never could've imagined Katie and I having a four-year-old daughter, me unknowingly marrying her sister, or me now having two kids whose life I wasn't a part of. My life was literally the complete opposite of what it used to be, and way beyond what I could've envisioned. I was alive though, and that's the reality I held onto, even when I felt like I was existing more than living. That's what I had to do for the moment because the moment I started to really live meant that I had to decide what to do about Honey. My sweet, treacherous, deadly Honey.

"Are you hungry?" Katie asked softly.

"I could eat."

After placing a quick kiss on my chest she tried getting up, but I pulled her back towards me until our lips touched. I blocked out all images and thoughts of Honey, and focused solely on Katie while kissing her with unchecked passion.

"Dollar, you don't—"

"Shhh, just put it on my face," I demanded hungrily, grabbing her by the hips.

I pushed her five foot three inch, one hundred fifty pound frame into the air like I was bench pressing a feather, and waited for her to grab ahold of the headboard. Once she did that, I guided her pussy down onto my face until I was wearing her like a mustache, and the feast began. I started out sucking on her clit until I could feel her whole pussy vibrating like an idling V-12 engine. I grabbed two handfuls of her all cheeks and forced her to ride my face while I alternated between licking and sucking.

"Oh shit," she moaned, when I let my teeth graze her clit.

When I bit down slightly, her body rocked and I quickly slid a finger into her asshole, while sucking her climax out of her. The wave of her cum threatened to drown me, but I fought against the current and drunk her like she was a 5-hour Energy drink. I didn't pull her down until the shaking in her body subsided to slight tremors, but I still gave her a moment to catch her breath while I held her against me.

"That n-never gets old," she stammered breathlessly.

"I'm glad, but if you got bored, I'm always open to bringing other women into the bedroom."

My comment earned me an elbow to the ribs, which made me chuckle. One huge difference between Katie and Honey was that she *did not* believe in sharing whatsoever. I wasn't mad for real, plus the fact that we didn't entertain other females helped us to keep a low profile. It hadn't been hard to stay off the radar since we'd both got shot, especially since everyone thought we were dead, but there was no need to risk exposure for some dumb shit. An eccentric rich couple that liked to swing definitely wouldn't go unnoticed in South Louisiana.

"Can I go cook us some breakfast now?" she asked.

I let my arms drop from around her, and she scooted off the king size bed.

"You might wanna put some clothes on because I think Denise and Savannah are off today," I said.

"It's okay, they've seen me naked before, and they said my body is better than my sister's."

I simply smiled as she pranced out of the room, choosing to keep my mouth shut about the lie the two women had told. I had no doubt they'd said it as a part of establishing where their loyalty lies. Savannah and Denise had saved both of our lives the night Honey had shot us and left us for dead. It had been luck on my part they'd both been staying in the house adjacent to my house while their condo was being renovated. Honey hadn't known that, and she also hadn't known that I owned the house next door, or above the underground tunnel that led to it. To this day, I don't know why I'd never told her about that particular escape route, but it turned out to save my life to have that secret. Because the cops had learned the hard way that my main house was booby trapped, it took them weeks to decide on a plan of action with regards to searching it. Infrared imaging told them no one was there, so in the end they chalked it up to Malcolm Joyner being extremely paranoid and rigging his house against some unknown attack. The authorities absolutely wanted to talk to him, even though it was almost impossible to prove those land mines hadn't been there since World War I or II. Thankfully, Savannah and Denise were a great doctor/nurse combo, and while they nursed us back to health right under the authorities' noses, I'd worked diligently to erase our existence. It hadn't been easy to do without Aubrey's help, but I couldn't let her know that I was alive without shit hitting the fan with Honey. I hadn't decided if I was gonna kill her, and I knew that until she had our baby that wasn't something I could even consider. So I'd made all four of us disappear setting up in an old mansion that I'd bought about six years earlier. It sat on ten acres so there was no one around to be nosey, and Denise and Savannah set up shop by volunteering at the local hospital, just like they had in Mississippi. As for Honey, well she'd disappeared, which enraged Katie for multiple reasons. It wasn't just the fact that Honey tried to kill her that had Katie upset, it was the fact that right now, she was playing mommy to the daughter Katie and I shared. That thought kept Katie and me up at night, but I was determined not to make a rash decision based on all the anger I felt. I'd been stalling Katie by making it clear that nothing and no one would harm Honey while she was pregnant, but now that we were in the tenth month of hiding, Katie was starting to push back. I didn't want to consider that possibility because that always forced me to remember the promise I'd made to keep her safe while she was pregnant. The truth I couldn't speak to Katie was that even though Honey had shot me and left me for dead, the loss of our first child was what prevented me from hunting her down. That loss had devastated both of us, and I carried too much guilt to put her through that again. Knowing she had to have given birth though changed shit. I mean, I couldn't *really* let her get away with trying to kill me, could I? I let that question accompany me to the bathroom, where I took a quick shower to ease the building tension that always came with contemplating Honey's fate. I wasn't a man who forgave the small shit, which meant forgiving big shit was out of the damn question. Yet to deny the love that I still felt even now for Honey was only me lying to myself. So could I forgive her? Did I truly want to, or did I just feel bad for betraying her with her own sister? One thing I know for sure was that I had too many questions and not enough goddamn answers! When I was finished with my shower, I threw on some clothes and followed the smell of eggs, sausage, and fried potatoes to the kitchen. I'd expected to find Katie cooking, but instead Denise was at the stove, and Savannah was looking down Katie's throat with a flashlight.

"What's wrong?" I asked.

"She was wheezing, and she sounded funny when she talked, so I decided to check her out real quick," Savannah replied.

Before I could offer up any reasonable explanations, I got a good look at Katie's neck and the fresh bruising in the shape of a large handprint.

"Just to be clear, that's not what it looks like," I said, pointing at Katie.

"Oh, so you didn't squeeze her throat while you two were fucking?" Denise asked innocently.

All eyes swung in my direction, but all I could do was shake my head and chuckle.

"I thought you would assume there was some domestic dispute so that's why I said—"

"We know you don't beat your women, Dollar. You may shoot them, but not beat them," Savannah said.

"True," Denise said, putting food on a plate.

I chose to leave the whole conversation alone and take a seat at the island across from the stove so I could watch Denise cook and the news at the same time.

"You're fine," Savannah declared, backing away from Katie.

"Told you that, but I appreciate your concern.

Well, since Denise has obviously kicked me off the stove I'ma grab a quick shower before breakfast," Katie said, kissing me on the cheek.

Out of habit I watched her juicy ass jiggle as she walked away before turning my attention back to the morning news. I was just about to change the channel when a news story about a terrorist attack in Amsterdam caught my attention, and forced me to turn the volume up to hear the report.

"Damn, it's not even safe to get pussy anymore," Denise said, shaking her head sadly.

I heard what she was saying, but I was more focused on the pictures of the scene. The famous Red-Light District was littered with rubble and cornered off by police tape. It was clear to see that one building took the brunt of the attack, but the cars that caught on fire made sure that no building went untouched. It could've very well been a planned terrorist attack as the news was claiming, and the excuse given about opposing sex trafficking could've been true. Something just didn't seem right. The minute a picture of multi-millionaire Jeffery Sentiles popped up on the screen, everything made sense instantly.

"That was a hit," I said confidently.

"A hit? Who the hell hits a whore house?" Savannah asked skeptically.

"Someone who knows that sex workers and people who patronize those establishments are easily forgotten after the initial shock wears off. It's a good place to take out a lot of people when one person was actually the target," I replied.

"You sound positive about that, Dollar," Denise said.

I was more than positive I was right in my assessment, but I hoped I was wrong about the feeling in the pit of my stomach. I could count on one hand the hittas who would use the tactic of taking out a group of people to get at one person, and I'd have fingers left over. This was definitely a job that I would take though, if I were *"alive"*. So who took the job since I was dead? It really shouldn't matter to me since I was halfway around the world, but I trusted my instincts, and right now they were screaming.

Aryanna

Chapter 3
Honey
St. Croix
Two days later

"It's good to have you back in one piece," Aubrey said, sitting across from me at the patio table. "There was never a doubt in my mind that that's how I'd return. I was trained by the best."

My response left us both silent as we travelled inside our own thoughts of Dollar. No doubt hers were full of love and laughter, while mine were filled with questions I would never get answers to. I did have a wealth of good memories to reflect on when it came to my late husband, but indulging in those always brought the guilt that I was trying to avoid. I didn't deserve to feel guilty because I wasn't the one who'd cheated.

"Did you peek in on the kids?" Aubrey asked.

"Yeah."

"Dorian looks more and more like his dad every single day, and I swear he had that same quiet power about him too. He's not like most babies who cry all day. I mean he does cry, but most of the time I feel like he's watching and waiting, even though I know that's impossible at his age."

Hearing this made me smile because even though it was highly impossible for my son to be analyzing the world around him at two months old, it wasn't impossible because of who his dad was. I would never put the limitations of the world on my son simply because I felt like his father was something that this world had never seen before. He was more than a man, and somehow, I knew he'd passed that on to his baby boy.

"How has Kyla been?" I asked.

"More or less the same, asking for her dad while sticking close to Dorian. She surprised me the other day by asking me about her mom though. She said I looked like her, and asked if I knew her."

For the first time since meeting Aubrey face to face I looked at her differently, trying to see what my niece saw. Aubrey was beautiful with lightly bronzed skin. She was probably about the same height as Katie, which put her at five feet three and a half inches, and she was thick, but toned, at one hundred forty-five pounds. That was where the similarities stopped though.

"You're physically built the same, but you're way more beautiful than my sister. Trust me."

"Well, thank you. I think Kyla is just missing both of her parents, and she doesn't understand why they haven't come back for her. Given your sister's long absence in Kyla's young life, I don't think it affects her as much as Dollar not being around does. I know they only got to spend a short time together, but her daddy became her whole world in that time, and now she just wanted that back."

"Don't we all," I said softly, looking out at the slowly rising sun through tear filled eyes.

My heart ached from the knowledge that I'd taken so much from those innocent kids that I claimed to love with all my heart. The internal struggle that I constantly battled was that I couldn't say with any connection that I would do shit differently if I had the chance. The saying went that hurt people hurt people, so I didn't know that I wouldn't pull the trigger all over again. The line between love and hate was *beyond* thin because sometimes that bitch was invisible. The feeling of hands on my shoulder's snapped me out of my current train of thought, as I offered my cheek for a kiss.

"When did you get back, Mama Honey?"

"A few hours ago," I replied.

"Why didn't you wake me up when you came in?"

"Because I knew that you had to be in school in a few hours Iree, and I'm not about to deal with phone calls about you falling asleep in someone's class," I said seriously.

"Facts," Aubrey chimed in.

"I'm appalled that you two would think I'd do something like that. I'll have you know that I *never* get caught sleeping in class."

"Ahhh, so you do sleep in class, but you just don't get caught," I said.

"My dad taught me that not getting caught is the same as not doing it," Iree replied, smiling.

Aubrey and I shared a knowing look, in part because we knew that Dollar was the only dad Iree had really known, and also because we knew that there was no undoing whatever lessons he'd instilled in her. Ever since Dollar had died, Iree had damn near become his doppelganger, which was part of the reason she'd refused to return to her life with her mom in Alabama. She would rather live a life on the run with me and her siblings to honor the memory of her "father," than to live a normal life. Even though she technically wasn't an adult because she was only seventeen, I still felt like it was her decision to make, and I supported it. Aubrey and I had taken her under our wings to give her all the game that we had between us, but only because she promised to give school the same amount of attention.

"I'm not even gonna waste my time arguing with you, Iree, and since you're up now I'm gonna assume you're ready for school," I said.

"Um, yeah…about that, I was thinking—"

"If you were thinking anything that don't involve you taking your ass to school today, I suggest you don't think it," Aubrey stated seriously.

"I can't go to school today. I've got something important to do."

"Like what?" I asked, looking up at her.

"I can't-I can't say."

"Oh, well then you *absolutely can't* do it. Sorry," Aubrey said sarcastically.

The look in Iree's eyes was begging for me to be the voice of reasoning and understanding, but I couldn't because I knew how Dollar felt about his kids education.

"I'm sure whatever it is can wait until after school," I said reassuringly.

Before Iree could respond the baby monitor in Aubrey's hand came alive with the sound of my son waking up.

"It sounds like he's hungry as hell the way he's sucking his thumb," I said, laughing.

"That's not his thumb, those are his toes in his mouth," Aubrey corrected.

For some reason that made me laugh harder as the visual of my son curled into a ball, gumming his own toes, popped into my mind.

"Let me find out that Dad passed a fetish on to him," Iree said.

I could feel the eyes of both women on me, and that only made me laugh harder still.

"That's just too much. Let me go get this boy," Aubrey said, rising from her chair and disappearing inside the house.

When Iree took the seat across from me I could tell that all traces of humor had vanished from her demeanor, and it gave me a feeling of instant anxiety.

"What's wrong, sweetheart?"

"Mama Honey, you know that I love Aubrey, but I trust you the most."

Hearing this should've made me feel warm and fuzzy, but instead it brought my guilt back to the surface with a quickness.

"I appreciate that, Iree, now tell me what's wrong."

"It's-It's school. The reason that I wasn't planning on going is because I needed to handle something with the P.E. teacher."

"Handle *what* with the P.E. teacher?" I asked, getting a bad feeling.

"He's-He's sick. I mean he's never done anything to me, but I know of at least two girls that he's pressured into sex. He had pull all over the island because his family has been here so long, and the girls were afraid that something would happen if they didn't give in. They came from working class families, and if their parents lost their jobs it would mean instant poverty."

"I understand sweetie, and that's *beyond* fucked up for that man to be preying on those children like that, but what were you planning to do?"

The look that she gave me said it all.

"Do you not feel like the authorities can handle this, Iree?"

"We never trust the authorities to handle shit, and you know that. Besides, with the pull of his family, and the fact that he's only twenty-six compared to the girls being seventeen, I'm not sure it's against the law here."

"Let me ask you something...are you one hundred percent positive that these girls didn't have sex with him because they wanted to?" I asked patiently.

"I'm positive. I didn't just take their word about what happened because I knew how this would turn out, so I investigated all the parties involved. Mama Honey, these are good girls, and they feel like they've had something taken from them."

I sat quietly and contemplated everything I'd just been told. Even though Dollar had killed at the drop of a dime, I had no doubts that he instilled in Iree the importance and seriousness of taking a life. Death was permanent, which meant that dishing it out needed to be heavily considered and reconsidered. I was all too familiar with the results when the due diligence wasn't done.

"So what was your plan?" I asked.

"I'd asked for one on one help so I could make the volleyball team, and he offered to tutor me privately at his house after school."

"What made you take that approach?" I asked curiously.

"Because that's how he came at the other two girls. He used the fact that his house accesses a private beach, and he'd demanded that they report there on different days and times because they were weighing the team down."

"Who does he live with, who knows about your appointment, and what have you told the girls that were assaulted?"

"He lives alone, nobody knows about my appointment, and I haven't done anything except be a supportive ear for both girls. They think I'm the nicest foreigner ever," she replied smiling.

I should've known that she would proceed cautiously, and without exposing her true objective. She may have technically been Dollar's sister, but he'd raised her and groomed her like any father would. He'd definitely be proud of the woman that she was becoming.

"Ok, I want you to give me all the info you have on dude, and I'll take care of it."

I'd expected to see relief on her face, but instead I saw hesitation and that made me more curious.

"Is there something that you're not telling me, Iree?'

"No, not really."

By her saying not really instead of no meant that there was definitely more to be said, so I sat still and patiently waited.

"It's just that this was something I wanted to take care of myself, Mama Honey. You and Aunt Aubrey can't take care of me forever."

"I understand that, I really do, and that's why we continue to do everything we can to prepare you for the world. It's what Dollar would've wanted. What he wouldn't have wanted was for you to get blood on your hands unnecessarily, and since I know that, I can't condone what you're suggesting. You know your dad, Iree, and he would never ever want you to be a cold-blooded killer."

When she looked away into the rising sun I could see the tears quickly filling her eyes, until they fell silently. Her obvious pain only intensified the guilt I felt for taking away the man that she loved the most, but like her I would suffer in silence. The emotional baggage that came with the decisions I'd made was mine to carry through life, and I accepted that. I used it as motivation to make the best decisions possible when it came to those that I loved because I refused to hurt them anymore, or let them hurt themselves.

"I know that you're right, Mama Honey...I miss Dad so much sometimes, and I wonder how I'm supposed to survive without him."

"You survive by knowing that he's never truly gone, sweetheart. He lives in every memory you have of him, and every lesson that he taught you."

"I was so fucking hardheaded though! There were times when I thought he was gonna give up on me, but he never did, not once. The crazy muthafucka shot me, but he didn't give up on me."

The memory her statement invoked made me chuckle because she was absolutely right. He'd shot her out of love, which would sound twisted to anyone who wasn't there that day. I'd witnessed the love Dollar had for his kids on more than one occasion, and I considered myself lucky for that. It hurt to know that I wouldn't get to witness that love between him and his son though, and some days I felt like I'd give anything to live in that moment. Wishing for that was pointless though, so all I could do was live life the way it was. This was what I wanted, right?

"I miss him just as much Re-Re, and I know that he's watching over us. That's why there's no way in hell I'ma let you take care of your perverted teacher on your own. I got you, you already know that, so run me that info before I get mad."

Her ability to smile through her tears made me feel slightly better and loosened the tightness that I'd been fueling in my chest. I took the cellphone that she handed me, and immediately started to go through it. I read the texts that her and Carlessio Pettycola had exchanged, and I was both amazed and disgusted by the boldness of this muthafucka. I truly had no interest in looking at the pictures he'd sent, but I needed to know how far this shit was going.

"Ewww!" I said, wishing I could unsee the world's tiniest dick pic.

"My thoughts exactly. I mean I don't know how he thought that shit would be sexy to anybody! The nigga has to piss on his nuts every time he goes to the bathroom."

The truth in that statement had me laughing out loud, but the sight of Aubrey coming back outside carrying my son made me tuck the phone away.

"I'll take care of it, and you can stay home from school until I do."

"Thanks, Mama Honey, I love you."

"I love you too."

She wiped the tears from her face, and moved around the table to give me a quick hug before she went back into the house.

"What's wrong with her?" Aubrey asked, reclaiming her seat.

I gave her a quick recap of our conversation while taking Dorian out of her arms, and covering his chubby cheeks with kisses.

"So what are you gonna do?"

"I'll handle it, just get me all the info that I need on him," I replied.

"It's risky taking care of business so close to home."

"I know, and that's why it has to look like an accident. I got this, Aubrey."

"Okay, I hear you. Speaking of work though, another suitable job offer came up. Are you interested?"

I took a moment to stare deeply into my son's eyes, and for a split second it was Dollar looking at me and smiling in that way that made me lightheaded. I took this as my sign.

"Yeah, I'm interested. I've got a lot more stress to relieve."

Chapter 4
Dollar

"Are you coming to bed, or were you planning on sitting in front of that laptop all night?" she asked.

I looked up from the screen in front of me to find a very naked Katie standing on the opposite side of my desk, holding a bowl of ice cream in her hand.

"What time is it?"

"A little after two a.m., which means that you've spent about thirty-six out of the last forty-eight hours in this office. You wanna tell me what's got your attention because it's *obviously* not me anymore," she said, pouting.

I took a moment to rub my eyes and sit back in my chair, while trying to decide how much I wanted to tell her. I knew that just mentioning Honey's name could be like lighting a stick of dynamite and holding it in my hand. The truth was that I'd let my curiosity get the best of me, and now I was certain that my other wife was attempting to fill my shoes. When we'd met, Honey had been a woman that had and would always survive by any means necessary. She was a survivor by any means necessary. She was a survivor. In the last thirty-six hours I'd learned that my sweet Honey had changed though, and now she was playing a game that wasn't simply about survival. She was chasing fulfillment.

"Close the door and sit down," I instructed.

While she did that I grabbed a pre rolled blunt from the box of them that I kept in my desk, and I lit it. As the smoke expanded my lungs my mind went back to analyzing the information that I'd uncovered. Honey had been careful in both her planning and execution, but I considered myself the best, which meant I'd known what to look for when I started digging around. Jeffery Sentiles had definitely been the target, and since I knew that Honey had no ties to him it was easy to conclude that she'd done it for business reasons. Being that I knew Aubrey would've given her access to the "in case" bank account I'd designed for Honey to live off of I also knew that she hadn't killed Jeffrey for money. She'd done it to heal something inside herself, and I knew all too well that no amount of killing could fill that hole. That meant if Honey wasn't careful she'd lose herself, and there were a couple reasons I couldn't allow that.

"Maybe we should have sex before we have this conversation because you look extremely tense," she said, flopping down in the chair across from me.

"Believe me, sex won't help. This is about Honey."

The flash in her eyes was the clearest indicator that the fuse to the dynamite was lit, but surprisingly she maintained her composure while eating a scoop of her cookies and cream ice cream.

"What about Tabitha?" she asked, putting emphasis on Honey's government name.

The change in her tone let me know to tread lightly because her aggressive side was obviously right around the corner and I didn't wanna deal with that.

"I think that she's in trouble, or about to be, and I might have to step in."

"Step in? As in help that bitch? You gotta be fucking joking Dameian, unless you've forgotten that part where she shot us both and left us to die."

"I didn't forget that, nor have I forgotten that she has our daughter. Her life and safety is more important than ours, and making sure that she's good is more important than revenge."

"What you're saying is true, but the fact that its coming out of your mouth right now is complete bullshit! For the last six weeks I've been asking you to get off your ass and make a move because that bitch had to have given birth by now, but you wouldn't budge. Oh, but now that you think your precious Honey is in trouble you wanna use the excuse of our daughters safety? That's some real lame nigga shit Dameian. I knew that my sister had made you soft, but damn I didn't think that she could turn you into a straight pussy."

I could smile as I continued smoking my blunt because I knew that Katie was intentionally trying to provoke me now. My right hand was itching fiercely to reach down into my desk drawer, grab the Glock 42 .380 I kept there, and spray her brain matter around the room like Febreze. I resisted the urge though because I knew that she was simply hurt and lashing out.

"I told you from the beginning that whatever happened to Tabitha would happen on my time, and according to my terms. So it doesn't matter what you've been trying to get me to do for the last month and a half because you don't run shit except your mouth. If you keep talking to me like that I'ma make it hard for you to run that muthafucka, and that's a promise."

Our staring contest only lasted a few moments before the ice cream in her bowl captivated her attention. The sight of silent tears sliding down her face made me feel somewhat bad, and forced me to change tactics because I didn't need to deal with an overly emotional female right now either.

"Listen Katie, I get why you're angry. I know that you got shot just like I did, but—"

"There is no but Dollar. Your gunshot wounds healed, but Tabitha murdered a part of me that day and I'll never get over that," she stated passionately.

Her words left me silent for a moment because I knew that there was nothing I could say to fix what was broken. When Honey and I had lost a baby we'd gotten through it together and found solace in the fact that we'd have another one day. This situation with her sister was different though because she hadn't lost a baby, she'd lost the ability to ever have one again. Savannah had to do a hysterectomy to save her life, and the cost of that was that she'd never naturally get pregnant or give birth again. I'd done my best to console her for the better part of this last year, but good dick and caring words couldn't change what had happened. Neither would killing Honey, but to Katie's way of thinking it would make them somewhat even.

"Come here," I said, putting my blunt out and pushing my chair back from the desk.

She hesitated briefly before putting her bowl on my desk, and coming around to sit on my lap.

"I can't understand the full extent of your pain because I didn't have to go through what you did, but I'm still sorry that you had to go through it. This situation is so fucked up and complicated that I haven't made a move simply because I didn't know which one to make. I've never been this undecided about anything in my life! The truth is that I feel like something has to be done at this point because Honey is showing signs that I find troubling, and I'm worried about our kids."

"What happened to make you worry?" she asked.

"I saw something on the news the other morning and it seemed weird to me, so I checked it out. It turns out that your sister was involved, and that makes me believe she's unstable right now."

"Be more specific Dollar, what's got you worried?"

While Katie and I had somehow ended up back together by default, I still wasn't about to forget that her actions were the catalyst to shit hitting the fan. She hadn't admitted to calling the cops on Honey for her crimes in Tennessee, but that was because I hadn't asked. I didn't need to ask when I knew the answer, and so for good reason I wasn't comfortable telling Katie that her sister had recently killed sixteen people in one night.

"What's got me worried is that Honey is not thinking or acting like a mother right now, and since she has two of my babies with her that's a problem for me," I replied truthfully.

"Ok, so what's you plan?"

"That's what I've been sitting here trying to figure out for the last twelve hours," I admitted.

"Well maybe you just need to take your mind off of it for a little while, and let the solution come to you."

Her suggestion made logical sense, but the way that she was touching me all over spoke to her motives of seduction.

"I guess taking a break won't hurt."

"But what if I want you to make it hurt?" she whispered in my ear, before biting down hard on my lobe.

As the air hissed from in between my teeth, I roughly grabbed her left tittie and pinched her nipple between my fingers until it was rock hard. When I moved her around in my lap so that she was straddling me, I took the taunt flesh of her nipple in between my teeth, and bit it just hard enough to make her gasp loudly. While she wrapped her arms around my neck to bring my face closer to her chest I was unzipping my shorts so that my dick could spring free. Like a heat seeker missile her pussy found what it wanted, and before I could brace myself she slammed down on me so that every inch was trapped inside her walls.

"Fuck this pussy," she demanded, kissing me hard.

As our tongues fought like bitter rivals my hands went to her firm ass cheeks, squeezing hard enough to leave fingerprints on her delicate skin while pulling her down hard on my dick. I could feel us both throbbing like dueling base drums by the third stroke, but I knew the fight was only beginning. When I stood up she locked her legs around my back, and that gave me more leverage to push up into her guts when I spun her into the wall right behind my chair.

"Fuck!" she exclaimed, holding onto me tighter as I tried to push her uterus through her back and the wall simultaneously.

The first wave of her orgasm allowed me to test the limits of her love cave, giving way to hidden walls that I pounded mercilessly. Our kisses took on the same savagery as our fucking, and suddenly I could taste blood in my mouth from us biting each other. That only served to throw kerosene on the already raging fire between us. I gave her long dick that forced the air from her lungs with every blow, but my kisses breathed new life into her. I could feel her body tense up in preparation for wave number two, and that made me fuck her faster. Within seconds her whole body rocked and bucked against me while her pussy clamped down on my dick hard enough to make me see stars on the backs of my eyelids. At the height of her orgasm I dropped her to her feet, spun her towards the wall, and mushed her face into the wood paneling while shoving my dick back inside her. I fucked her with an animals intensity until I felt my climax coming. I grabbed a handful of her hair and pulled it hard enough to detach it from the root as I worked my dick inside her tight asshole.

"Y-you won't last two m-minutes," she taunted, throwing that ass back at me.

I made sure to bounce her forehead off the wall with each stroke, while fighting against the death grip that her asshole was putting on me. I had every intention of making it last just to prove a point, but she made it impossible for me not to cum and I was forced to surrender before I had ten good strokes in. I came so hard that I lost my balance and we tumbled to the floor, laughing hysterically.

"That's-that's what you get for trying to give me a concussion," she said smiling at me.

"It was w-worth it."

We laid on the carpet looking at each other until the afterglow faded, and our minds synchronized around the same thought. Honey.

"Whatever you plan I need to be a part of it, Dollar."

"In what way?"

"In every way. Kyla is my daughter too, so whatever rescue mission you have in mind I need to be down with. Of course you already know that I need to be there when you kill that bitch too," she replied smiling.

I hoped that my eyes didn't reveal my indecision about whether I actually planned on killing Honey or not because I didn't feel like fighting with Katie. The honest truth was that I didn't know if I was gonna kill her. I didn't know if I could kill her, even though she'd tried to kill me. If anybody should be able to understand my indecision it should be the woman laying next to me since I'd tried to kill her before, but I knew that there were too many emotions for her to see the parallels. This was a call that I'd have to make on my own because I had to live with the consequences forever.

"I got you. I've still got some more research to do so that I can find her present location, and then we can plan from there."

"Okay. Don't stay up to long though because I'll be in bed waiting on our next round," she said, kissing me quickly before standing up.

I waited until she'd retrieved her bowl of melted ice cream and left before I got off the floor, and sat back at my desk. My body felt less tense, but my mind was still trying to attack the problem I was facing to find an adequate solution. After I relit my blunt, I got back to work by hacking into the database of the authorities in Amsterdam to see if there was any mention of Tabitha Dewitt. It only took me fifteen minutes to go through the file they'd put together for the attack on the Redlight district, and when I was done I could feel myself smiling. They had no *idea* that one of the deadliest attacks in their recent history had been carried out by a beautiful little woman with a bad temper. I couldn't help but feel pride for what she was able to accomplish, but that didn't change my opinion about stopping her. For Honey to kill for any other reason than direct survival for her or those that she loved meant that she was mentally in bad space, and that made me question my kid's safety. I was sure that I could've contacted Aubrey and she would give me Honey's exact location, but if I did that I was taking the chance that

Honey would know I was coming. I had no doubt that her and Aubrey had gotten close, and if Aubrey suddenly distanced herself then Honey would become suspicious. To avoid that I decided to track her the old fashion way by monitoring her family. With her being wanted for two counts of capital murder I knew she wouldn't be in the U.S., but she'd still set up a way for her parents and kids to contact her. My first move was to check the kids social media following, and that's when shit got real. As soon as I saw the poster on Ray's page my mission and focus shifted entirely, and I got to work with a surgeon's precision. I had been hoping that the poster saying that Rain Dewitt was missing was a bad joke between brother and sister, but within minutes I was reading the police report filed by a detective in Tuscaloosa, Alabama. According to it, my stepdaughter had been missing for almost two days, and had been last seen at school. I gathered all the information I could, and then I waited. After an hour ticked slowly by I crept upstairs where I found a softly snoring Katie sprawled naked across the bed. As quietly as I could I changed clothes, loaded my three favorite guns into my small travel bag with ammo and silencers, grabbed some cash, and quickly wrote Katie a note. Five minutes later, I was behind the wheel of my 2020 Mercedes AMG 565 Coupe speeding off into the darkness, preparing to unleash terror once again.

Chapter 5
Honey
One day later

"How are you doing beautiful?"

"I'm fine, how about yourself," I replied, smiling at the young man approaching me.

"Oh I'm a lot better now that I can see you're not a mirage."

I giggled girlishly at his lame line while waiting on him to close the distance between us on the beach.

I knew that a scantily clad, beautiful woman, watching the sunset on a private beach all alone would be too much of a temptation for Carlessio Pettycola to resist. The fact that I looked like I was in my late teens to early twenties only further worked to my advantage when it came to the fishing expedition I was on. Once Aubrey had dug a little deeper into Carlessio's past we found out that Iree had been more right than she knew because when Carlessio was nineteen he was charged for sexual assault against a girl that was under thirteen years old. So his exploits in sexually predatory behavior hadn't just started with the high school girls he was hired to work with, he was a seasoned pervert. His family money and power kept his dirty little secrets hidden, and made him feel like he was untouchable, but he was about to find out how mistaken he was.

"I can tell by your accent that you're not from the island so what brings you to our slice of paradise?" he asked, taking a seat beside me in the sand.

"I'm on vacation with my family."

"And where are your family members?" he asked looking around.

"Back at the hotel. I just needed a moment to myself so that I could enjoy the islands beauty on my own."

"There's a lot of beauty to be seen, if you're open to it."

The fact that he scooted closer to me as he spoke only made his innuendo impossible to misunderstand, but I still gave him my best innocent look and smile.

"How long have you lived here?" I asked.

"I'm born and raised here sweetheart. In fact, my family dates back to the first settlers of the island, so my bloodline is pure St. Croix."

"Wow, I bet you have a lot of stories you could tell since you have such a rich history here," I said, making sure to give him my brightest smile.

"I surely do. Would you like to hear some of them?"

"Sure, I mean if you don't have anywhere to be right now. I didn't tell my family when to expect me back, so I've got time if you do."

The smile he gave me after hearing this reminded me of the wolf in little red riding hood, but it didn't shake me. Poor thing didn't realize that he was now the prey.

"I don't have anywhere to be, and as your luck would have it my house is just through the bushes over there. You see the cottage with those lights on?"

My gaze followed in the direction that he was pointing, and I made the appropriate sounds of being impressed by what I could see.

"It's nice, but…well, I don't wanna intrude or impose on you or anyone you live with, I said.

I knew that he'd heard the question before he spoke.

"You're not imposing or intruding because I live all alone. I actually don't entertain at my house, but I've got some artifacts that were passed down to me through the generations and I think you'll find them interesting."

I gave the appropriate amount of pause to represent contemplation before I finally smiled, and nodded my head in acceptance of his invitation. He quickly stood up, and offered me his hand.

"Such a gentlemen, but you know I just realized that I don't know your name," I said, smiling sheepishly at him.

"I go by Monkey man."

The laughter that sprang from my mouth was genuine and heart felt because when I looked at him I suddenly saw his resemblance to his primate lineage. I tried to get it together, but the nigga really did look like a young baboon.

"It's good to see that you have a great sense of humor because I've got some jokes that are guaranteed to have you in tears before the nights over."

He spoke these words with a smile on his face, but even through the tears I could see the sinister twinkle in his eyes.

"I love to laugh," I replied, looping my arm through his.

I could feel the confidence in his steps as we made our way up the beach towards his cottage. Once we reached the bushes we came to a path that was too narrow to walk side by side, so he was forced to lead the way. I used the cover of night, and the fact that he was in front of me, to put a reassuring hand on the pistol secured in the back of my shorts. I was hoping that I wouldn't have to shoot him, but if he acted stupid that was his one way ticket home. When I saw that the path actually led to his back door, I quietly pulled the HK VP 9mm pistol out, and made sure the safety was on.

"This place is beautiful Monkey man."

"Wait till you see the inside," he replied, opening the door and stepping aside for me.

The smile on his face vanished like he'd smelled a fart when he saw the gun I was holding.

"Wh-what's this?" he asked hesitantly.

"I'll gladly explain once we're inside Carlessio. I promise you that I won't shoot you unless you make me, but if you do what I tell you this will be over quick *and* we'll still have sex."

Before he could say anything I unbuttoned my shirt and made the sign of the cross over my heart. Of course all he was paying attention to was my lack of bra, and how perky my tits were.

"O-ok," he said, licking his lips before turning to go inside.

I swiftly moved up behind him and smacked him viciously over the head with the pistol, knocking him unconscious. I quickly closed and locked the door before putting the pistol back in my shorts, and pulling two zip ties out of my pocket. After securing his hands and feet I dragged his gorilla looking ass into the nearest bedroom that I could find. I made my way quickly through the cottage, making sure that we were actually alone, while locking his front door and all the windows I could find. I didn't want anyone interrupting us while we were fucking. On the way back to the bedroom I grabbed the sharpest knife that I could find, and a bottle of rubbing alcohol. Since he was still sleeping peacefully I decided to set the stage. I got Carlessio on the bed face down, and cut his shorts and boxers clean off. I emptied my pockets and stripped off my clothes before tying a bandanna around my face to conceal all except my eyes, and the curly wig I was wearing. Once that was done I propped my cellphone up on his dresser in a way that got the perfect angle of the bed, and then I pulled on the eight inch strap-on dick that I'd had concealed next to my pistol. When I looked down at the fake dick protruding from my body, I thought about how painful it was gonna be for him to take every inch of it. That made me smile, but it also made me realize that I'd neglected a few details that were important to the success of this whole operation. I quickly went in search of extra sheets and some tape, luckily finding both within a matter of minutes. I looped the sheets through his arms and secured them to the polls of his canopy bed, and then I stuffed one of his socks in his mouth so that I could cover it with duct tape. I stepped back to observe my handy work, and once I was satisfied I pressed record on my phone and I climbed on top of him.

"It would be rude not to use any lubrication, Monkey man, so I got you," I said, pouring some rubbing alcohol down the crack of his ass.

I made sure to put some on the strap-on too, and then I flipped the switch that turned on the rotating clit stimulator that vibrated on my side of the toy. My pussy started to throb instantly under the steady vibrations, and that was all the motivation necessary for me to get the party started. I made sure the dick was aligned perfectly with his asshole, and then I put my back into the stroke that stole his virginity.

"What the fuck?" he mumbled around his gag, struggling against his restraints.

"Just relax Monkey man, you're kind of tight now, but I got you."

I eased back slowly without pulling all the way out of him, and then I slammed the dick back in him.

"Ahhhh!" he squealed, trying to run and back me off at the same time.

I held on tight though, enjoying the sensations shooting through my body from the attention my clit was getting as much as I was the pain Carlessio was enduring. I added a little more rubbing alcohol to the mix which made his muffled screams go up an octave, but I didn't give a fuck because no one could hear him, and he deserved this action. I fucked him without mercy for five solid minutes until I came, and then I finally pulled the strap on all the way out of him. The smells of shit and blood filled the air as turds fell out of his ass and onto his bed.

"Looks like I fucked the shit out of you, huh?" I asked, chuckling.

There was no witty reply or string of curse words, just the sounds of a broken man sobbing real tears. I climbed down off the bed, and moved around to where I could look him in the eyes.

"Do you know why this happened Carlessio?"

I could tell by the look of utter devastation in his eyes that he didn't wanna talk, but he still managed to shake his head no.

"This happened because you chose to prey on young girls. You chose to force them to have sex with you, so in essence you raped them because you took away their free will. I felt like you needed to know what that felt like. Do you get it now Carlessio?"

I hadn't really expected any type of contrition, but the look of pure hatred and rage told me that he wasn't as broken as I wanted him to be. Without a word I climbed back on the bed, got behind him, and shoved the hard plastic dick in him as far as it would go. I let his grunts and cries motivate me to the point that I was literally fucking him like I missed him. When I came again from the strap on rubbing my clit I didn't stop, I simply fucked him harder than before. It was the longest twenty minutes of his life before I finally stopped. Instead of pulling the dick out of him though I unhooked it from the harness and left it in him as I got off the bed. When I looked in his eyes this time I recognized the look he was giving me as that of a person who's lost their foothold on reality. I left him laying just like that and I went to take a shower. When I was done I stopped the recording on my phone, and started the process of cleaning up all the evidence of my presence, which meat I finally had to pull the dildo out of him. I laughed while doing it as the thought crossed my mind that he really did look like a Monkey man with a pink ass. I borrowed a grocery sack to put all my stuff in, got dressed, then went in search of any accelerants I could find. I went from room to room dosing everything in sight with liquor, making sure to save his bedroom for last so that my escape route wasn't blocked. I made sure to smack him over the head with my pistol hard enough to render him unconscious again, and then I cut his zip ties off him. Just to make sure that he didn't make a run for it I cut his achilleas on both legs before setting the blaze. My exit was quiet and I took the sane path that I'd arrived by, strolling leisurely down the beach until I came to where I'd parked my scooter. By the time that I'd made it to the main road the night sky was alive with the glow from a monstrous fire, but I puttered right on past it without so much as a glance. A half an hour later I had disposed of all incriminating evidence except for the video on my phone, and I stopped for a bite to eat at an outdoor café. I took my time enjoying my bowl of beef stew while going over what had happened in my mind to make sure that I hadn't made any mistakes. It was moments like this that made me appreciate the time that I'd had with Dollar in a different way because he'd taught me the importance of over analyzing. I searched every corner of my brain until I felt comfortable with what I'd done, then I paid my check and got back on my scooter. The ride back to my house didn't force me to go back past Carlessio's, but I took the scenic route just to check shit out. I wasn't disappointed to see the fire department trying their damnedest to contend with the blaze that was still raging, but I managed to keep a straight face as I drove by. I arrived home twenty minutes later with the intentions on enjoying a quiet evening at the house with the kids, but to my surprise all I found was a note from Aubrey saying that she'd taken them out to eat. I wasn't sure what to do with a house to myself, but I knew that my bottle of patron would keep me company. I was just about to go outside when sounds from deeper in the house caught my attention, forcing me to pull my pistol out so that I could investigate. I could've sworn that I was hearing voices, but as I moved down the hallway the sounds became nothing more than mumbles. I rounded the corner with my gun out in front, safety off, and my finger on the trigger only to find Iree in a vicious lip boxing match with a girl. I wasn't upset until I got a good look at the girl she was kissing in the moonlight.

"What the fuck are you doing?" I asked, startling both.

"Oh, uh, hi Mom."

Chapter 6
Dollar
Alabama

The restless thinking going on inside my head had me considering that maybe I was too out of practice for the game of hunting, but I had to trust that my instincts would get me through. So far I hadn't been able to pick up Rain's trail, and the fact that I'd only been in Alabama for half a day wasn't a valid excuse in my mind. I'd found more exclusive people quicker, which meant that I was rusty after my ten-month layoff. The fact that I didn't have Aubrey behind me played a part too, but my cyber stalking skills came second to no one so I couldn't lean on that excuse. All I could do was stay focused, and that was what had me sitting outside of Rain's best friend's house contemplating how I wanted to approach her. True enough she was a kid, and a good kid based on all that I'd been able to dig up on her, but if she stood between me and *my kid* then we had a problem. Rain was as much my daughter as Iree and Kyla, despite the fact that her mom had shot me, so her safety was my top priority right now. After grabbing my Ruger .45 from my bag and screwing on the silencer I calmly stepped out of my car, and tucked the gun in the waist of my jeans. I'd lost some weight since the shooting, but at 6'3", 210lbs I was still an imposing figure not to be fucked with or tested. I walked straight up to the front door, rang the bell, and waited. I could hear movement and the sound of a dog barking in the distance, and a few moments later a short, attractive white woman opened the door.

Aryanna

"May I help you?" she asked politely.

"I need to speak with Alex."

"Alex? As in my sixteen-year-old daughter Alex?" she asked, looking at me a little less hospitable than a moment before.

"If you're Alex's mom, then yes we're talking about the sane girl. I'm Rain's dad."

"But you're black," she blurted out.

"You think?" I asked sarcastically, looking down at my hands.

"I-I'm sorry, I didn't mean to be rude. It's just that I've known Rain for years, and even though she's definitely too thick to be all white, I didn't know that her dad was black."

"Well I am, just like Alex's dad."

My comment about her own daughters fixed heritage didn't seem to shock her as much as it put her in her place, but I didn't really give a fuck. I didn't have time for Alabama politics or backwoods bullshit. I needed to find Rain.

"The police already talked to Alex about where Rain could be, and she told them everything that she knows. She loves Rain like a sister."

"I believe that, but to be perfectly honest with you I'm not the type of father to sit around and wait on the cadaver dogs to find my child. I'll find her first, and she'll be alive and unharmed. In order for that to happen I'm gonna need to speak with your daughter."

For a moment she simply stared back at me and I almost believed that she was ready to meet Jesus, but she suddenly called her daughter's name and summoned her to us. A few moments later a familiar face from Rain's Instagram and Facebook pictures stepped into view, looking back and forth between me and her mom. Alex was much more beautiful in person with her curly black hair and high yellow skin tone, and there was no doubt that she would grow into a gorgeous woman. If she lived that far.

"Yes mama?"

"Alex, this is Rain's dad and he wants to talk to you about her. I'll be right here with you so—"

"I'm okay mom I'll talk to him by myself," Alex said, looking me directly in the eyes.

For a moment her mom hesitated, but then she reluctantly stepped back into the house and left us on the front porch.

"Your mom seemed surprised when I said that I was Rain's dad, but you're not. Why is that?" I asked curiously.

"Because Rain told me about you when she came back from vacation in Mississippi. I thought you were dead though?"

"Yeah, that's what a lot of people thought, including Rain probably. As you can see I'm not dead though, and I'm looking for my daughter, which brings me to your door step this evening. So Alex, where's Rain?"

"I don't know. I haven't seen her since third period three days ago," she replied.

Even though I knew that Alex was a friend to Rain I still scrutinized her the way that I would anyone else I suspected of lying to me. Luckily for Alex I was sure that she was telling me the truth. Unfortunately I knew instinctively that there was more to the story.

"So what did Rain tell you about me?" I asked.

"Nothing much, just that you're some kind of investment broker or something and you have a lot of money."

"I do have a lot of money, but I didn't make it through investments. I'll tell you how I made it if you promise me that you can keep a secret."

"I promise," she said, raising her right hand like we were in court.

I motioned for her to come closer to me, and then I leaned in so that I was inches away from her ear.

"I kill people for money, and I'm really good at it," I whispered.

When Alex pulled back I could see the disbelief swimming in her brown eyes, but just beneath that was curiosity. When I pulled up my shirt so that she could see the butt of my gun those eyes suddenly lit up with excitement, and just as quickly the reaction that I'd expected settled right in. Fear.

"I won't lie to you Alex at times I'm not a nice person because the world isn't a nice place. Right now someone that I love very much is out there in this world, and I need to make sure that she's alright, which means I'm perfectly fine with not being nice. Do you understand where I'm coming from?"

"Y-yes I get it."

"Good, so let me ask you one more time just to be sure. Where is my daughter?"

"I r-really don't know, but-but you should ask her ex-boyfriend Jermarlyn," she replied nervously.

"Okay Alex, I can do that. Is there anyone else that I should ask?"

"N-no, just ask him."

I locked eyes with her in a way that conveyed how bad of an idea it would be for her to withhold any information from me. Once I was convinced that she would've told me all of her secrets before ever uttering a lie I nodded my head for her to go inside, and she quickly disappeared. I made my way back to my car, got in, and headed to the next address on my list. It just so happened to be Rain's ex-boyfriend. From all outward appearances he seemed to be a nice boy, but from personal experience I knew that teenage boys weren't shit because they were motivated by one thing. Sex. I already had it in my mind that this conversation was about to go a whole lot differently than the one I'd had with Alex just because this little muthafucka had dated my daughter. He was about to get the same treatment as any nigga that Iree was fucking with. When I pulled up at his house twenty minutes later under the cover of darkness I spotted his dark blue sixty-seven old school Chevy Nova parked on the grass. While I was going over the approaches to take in my mind lady luck smiled on me in the form of the six foot, stocky seventeen-year-old kid I'd seen in pictures on Rain's Facebook page appearing like magic. He stepped out of his house and was headed in the direction of his car, which made my decision easy for me. I hopped out with my gun in hand, and strolled up on him with a purpose to my movements.

"Let's take my car," I said, pointing the gun at his broad chest.

"Wh-what?"

"Just do as I say Jermarlyn and you'll be fine."

I could tell that the fact that I knew his name scared him more than the hand cannon I was pointing at him, but he still didn't move until I pulled the slide on my pistol and chambered a round.

"What-whatever this is about can be worked out," he said, putting his hands up in the air.

"Oh, I have no doubts about that Jermarlyn, just get in the passenger seat and take a ride with me."

We both made our way to my car, and once he got in I followed his lead. I kept the gun in my left hand in my lap while putting the car in gear and navigating with my right, wondering if this young boy would make the mistake of thinking that he could take me.

"I know you're big and fast because you play football, but you ain't faster than a bullet so if you do some dumb shit your brains will beat all coherent thought out of that side window. If you tell me what I wanna know then this won't hurt, but if you don't..."

I let the rest of my sentence trail off to make my point clear.

"What d-do you wanna know?"

"Where's Rain Jermarlyn?"

"Who?"

I didn't let my anger at his response show, and I only spared him a brief glance as I continued to drive. I didn't ask another question, and he kept his mouth shut despite the rising tension that I could feel rolling off of him in waves. It probably seemed like I was driving around aimlessly to him after ten straight minutes of twists and turns, but when we pulled up back at his house I could see the confusion in his eyes.

"Are your parent's home?" I asked.

"Y-yeah, why?"

"Let's go have a chat with them," I replied, turning off the engine, and putting the key in my pocket.

I stepped out of the car, and motioned with my pistol for Jermarlyn to follow me. It was almost comical that he was showing more hesitation now than when I'd forced him into my car, but he eventually got out and led the way to his front door.

"I'm just grabbing my keys" he said, reaching slowly into his pocket.

I watched his every move like the seasoned killer that I was, ready to sever his spine with a well-placed bullet without hesitation or remorse. It took him four tries to actually get the key in the lock and open the door for us to enter, but his nervousness was understandable at this point. I followed him through the door that opened to a living room on our left and a set of stairs leading to the second floor on our right. An older black couple was sitting on the couch watching T.V, and just at a glance I could tell that these were Jermarlyn's parents.

"Did you forget something son?" the man asked.

"Apparently he forgot his ex-girlfriends name, but I'm sure that we can jog his memory," I said, closing the door behind me.

I swiftly leveled my gun at the still confused older man, and all that you heard was the soft cough come from my barrel as the gun came alive. Pink and gray brain matter splattered the floral wallpaper pattern in a display of artistic beauty. The scream that erupted from the throat of Jermarlyn's mom was short lived, and never got to reach its full potential because I shook my head at her, and she took the hint. The speed with which Jermarlyn spun around and took a step forward to advance towards me was a thing of beauty, but it still wasn't quick enough to avoid the hot slug I put in his knee cap. The way he attacked the floor wasn't graceful at all, but I did admire the fact that he didn't try to beg and plead.

"Now when we were in the car I asked you where Rain was, and you played dumb. I should've explained that I'm her dad, and I wouldn't be here unless I knew to fucking be here, so I'm gonna ask you again. Jermarlyn, where's my daughter?"

"I-I don't know, I swear! She's wherever her mom is!"

"Explain that statement," I demanded.

"She-she wasn't kidnapped or anything, she ran away to be with her m-mom."

"Did you help my daughter run away?" I asked calmly.

"I-I just gave her money."

"You shouldn't have," I said, shooting him in the other knee cap.

Before he could scream I took aim at where I thought his dick was and fired two shots. The sudden change in his voice mid scream let me know that my aim was still worthy of any branch of the United States armed services. Without a word I turned the gun back on his mother, and added her thought pattern to her husband with one tap of the trigger. I stood over Jermarlyn and let him scream until his voice finally cracked and quit on him. I could see that he was bleeding out very fast, which meant that he'd probably die before anyone had the chance to save him. I didn't live my life on probabilities though when it came to death because death had to be certain, and inescapable. I fired two bullets into Jermarlyn's forehead to make sure that he understood that lesson. After a quick survey of my handy work I made sure to wipe my prints off the front door before using a handkerchief to open and close it on my way out. My stroll back to my car was casual so as not to draw attention to myself, and within moments I was a ghost once again. It took me half an hour to make it back to my motel, and once I was there I came face to face with the question of what my next move should be. If Rain was with Honey then she was safe, but the question remained had she made it to wherever Honey was yet? How was she travelling, and who was she trusting? There was no doubt in my mind that Honey had known Rain was coming she wouldn't have let her parents involve the cops, so that meant that more than likely she was in the dark about our impulsive daughter. That would mean that Rain's only ally in this situation was Iree. That logical thought led me to my laptop because now I knew what blind alley to run down in search of answers. I set up shop on the hard mattress that passed for a bed, and ordered me some food so that I could get to work. An hour and a half, two cheeseburgers, and an order fries later I'd found exactly what I was looking for, which left me with the only question of what to do now? Was I really ready to face Honey and our past?

Aryanna

64

Chapter 7
Honey

"Rain Mckenzie Dewitt, what the fuck are you doing here?" I asked in a low growl.

"Your middle name is Mckenzie?" Iree asked.

The look I turned on her made her shut her mouth immediately because now was not the time for any dumb shit.

"Geez Mom, I thought you would've been missing me as much as I miss you, but—"

"Don't you *dare* try that shit with me Rain because you know that I miss you, but you also know that it's not safe to be around me because I'm on the run. You fucking know that too Iree Grace Blevins!" I stated angrily.

"Your middle name is Grace?" Rain asked.

The way that they smiled at each other would've been cute, if it didn't make me wanna shoot the both of them.

"Yeah, I can really tell that you came all this way to see me Rain," I said sarcastically.

Her smile instantly vanished and I could see the hurt in her eyes clearly in the moonlight.

"Mom if this was about Iree she could've just came home to Alabama because she's not wanted for two counts of capital murder. I wanted to see you. I needed to see you because I couldn't keep living with the thought of never seeing you again unless it was on the news or in a coffin. I love you mommy."

Her words pushed my tears from their hiding place, and before I knew it I had her in my arms and we were sobbing together. I don't even resist when Iree took the pistol from my hand and left us alone, I just hugged Rain tighter while inhaling her familiar scent. It took us a long time to get our emotions under control, but that was okay because I felt like my soul needed to feel what it was feeling in this moment. God knew that I needed my daughter as much as she needed me, and that's why he'd brought us back together.

"How the hell did you get here?" I asked, pulling back so that I could look down at her.

"That's a long story Mom."

I took her by the hand and led her into the kitchen where I found Iree making a turkey sandwich.

"How did you two pull this off?" I asked her.

"Well, once she slipped away from your parents I sent a car for her that took her to Florida, and from there she hopped on a plane to the Bahamas. After that it was nothing more than a boat ride and a taxi," Iree replied.

I shook my head and tried not to be too frustrated, while trying to remember that I was dealing with two impulsive teenagers.

"This wasn't smart Iree. If the Feds traced her movements then they could be here any minute, and that puts us all I danger."

"Hiding out in a territory owned by the U.S. wasn't smart, but here we are right? Plus I'ma need you to give me a little more credit than that too because you and Aubrey have taught me well. Travelled using cash, the plane was chartered through one of dad's legit business identities, and the boat that brought her here is owned by people who don't ask question. We're good Mama Honey."

I was actually impressed that my sixteen and seventeen year old girls had been able to put together a workable escape plan so quick, but I wasn't about to tell them that right now.

"You still know the rules about going rogue," I said, pointing at Iree.

"I do, and that's why I made sure to take this from you," she replied, lifting up her shirt to show me the butt of my own gun.

I tried to keep a straight face, but the laughter in my throat wouldn't be denied so I had to let it out.

"Well played baby girl," I said.

The sound of the front door opening grabbed all of our attention, and before I could blink Iree had the gun out and levelled in that direction. We both recognized the familiar sound of Kyla's voice at the same time, which allowed us to relax. A few moments later Aubrey and Kyla came around the corner with Dorian's carrier in between them. Kyla was oblivious to Rain and the rest of us because she was having a full conversation with her baby brother, but Aubrey spotted her immediately and looked straight at me with a question.

"It's a long story, but its ok I think. I'll tell you about it in a minute, but first things first, we have to make introductions," I said, turning to Rain.

"Would you like to meet your newest little brother?"

I don't know how she'd take the news of me having another baby, but her sudden gasp followed by a smile full of tears made me breathe easier. She walked slowly over to the carrier and peeked at my smiling bundle of joy. This got Kyla's attention immediately, and I chuckled as she protectively stepped in front of Dorian and sized Rain up.

"It's okay Kyla, she's family," I said.

"What's her name mom?" Rain asked.

I could tell that her calling me mom got Kyla's attention immediately.

"That's your mom?" Kyla asked, looking at Rain while pointing at me.

"Yes, that's my mom."

It was fascinating watching Kyla input this information into her brain because the emotions of confusion and protectiveness were written all over her face. After a few moments she stepped aside so that Rain could see her little brother.

"That's Dorian. He's my little brother. Is he your brother too?" Kyla asked.

"Yes he is, but I don't know him so can you introduce us?" Rain asked.

"Sure."

Kyla's smile was wide and beautiful as she took on the role of proud big sister and told Rain who Dorian was. I nodded at Aubrey for her to put the carrier down, and follow me outside so that we could talk.

"You know that Kyla doesn't like to share, right?" Aubrey asked.

"Yeah I know, but they'll be fine."

Once we were seated around the patio table I ran down my entire evening to Aubrey, making sure to speak in a low tone so that our voices wouldn't carry back inside. A few times I could hear the kids laughter, and it gripped my heart in a bittersweet way because I wished that their dad could hear that sound.

"So what's your plan for your daughter?" Aubrey asked.

"Honestly I don't know, but right now I'm feeling like the worst mother in the world for having all these kids with me while I'm on the run."

"I admit that its risky, but any fool with eyes can see how much you love those children in there. I can only imagine how hard it is to look at Dorian because he's the mirror image of his dad, but you've still managed to push through and perceiver. You're a good mom Honey, but now you have to make the tough decisions that come with that."

Aubrey's words of truth lessened the confusion in my heart, but it didn't make my decision any easier. I had fond memories of raising my two oldest kids, and of us really growing up together in a way. I wanted those same memories with my younger children now, but I didn't know how to accomplish that goal if I was constantly looking over both shoulders.

"I think that I need to leave St. Croix," I said.

"Wherever you go we're gonna follow you," Iree stated.

Her voice had come out of the darkness, starling Aubrey and I, and when we turned towards it I could just make out Iree's silhouette amongst the shadows.

"It's impolite to eavesdrop," I said.

She came out of the darkness and sat down at the table next to me.

"I wasn't trying to eaves drop Mama Honey, I was actually coming to talk to you about that problem we discussed, and I overheard what you said. I'm telling you now that I'm not letting you leave us, and don't try to make it sound like it's for our own good either because it's not. We need you for our own good."

"Sweetheart I know that you feel that way, but you're not thinking about what happens if I get caught or caught up out here in these streets. All of you kids will be taken from me, and put only god knows where! I can't allow that Iree, and you know damn well that Dollar would kill me for putting any of you in danger," I replied.

"Dollar ain't here, and you're all we got. I need you to think about that Mama Honey before you try dumping us off on anybody."

I could hear the pain in her voice, but she didn't give me time to defend my logic before she got up from the table and walked back into the house.

"You ok?" Aubrey asked softly.

"I don't know what the fuck to do Aubrey! I wish...god, I need Dollar so much sometimes, and it fucking rips my heart out because I know he—"

"You know he what?" she asked, when I didn't finish.

I'd been about to say that I knew he didn't love me because he was still fucking my sister, but that secret was mine to take to the grave too. The truth of it had tears pouring from my eyes though as I stared off into the night. I think the part that haunted me the most was that I still didn't know why he'd done me like that. Could it really all have been a lie between us? The prospect of that being true hurt more than when I'd killed him, but I'd have to live with this pain until it was my time to die.

"Let's talk about something different," I said, pulling my phone out and passing it to her.

I could tell by her laughter when she'd started watching the video, but she didn't bother looking at the whole thing.

"I noticed the fire department working in vain when I was coming home, so I take it Carlessio is no more?"

My smile was all the response she needed.

"Well sis, you've had a long day so why don't we put these kids to bed, and get some sleep," she suggested, handing me my phone back.

"You read my mind."

We went back into the house prepared to move as a united front, but the sight of all the kids huddled together on the floor melted our hearts, and resistance. I know that Iree was more than capable of handling Dorian and Kyla, so once I made sure that my little man had enough bottles made I took my ass to bed. Part of me wanted to pray for a good night's sleep, but I knew it would be a wasted prayer, so I settled in for the inevitable. To my surprise my eyes were closed almost as soon as my head hit the pillow, and for the first time in almost two and a half months I slept a dreamless sleep. The fact that I hadn't woken up with the cold sweats or eyes puffy from crying during the night shocked me enough to cause me to lay in my bed as the sun's orange glow lit my curtains with warm color. I knew that I was waiting for all the bricks of emotion and guilt to hit me in the chest, but as the seconds turned to minutes it seemed like I was waiting in vain. I climbed slowly from my bed and went to my shower so that I could stand under the water spray, and cry. The tears didn't seem so heavy on this particular morning, and before I knew it they'd stopped leaking from my eyes. Not wanting to tempt whatever good fortune was allowing me to breeze through my ritual of grief made me skip my morning orgasm, and end my shower after washing myself. By the time I got out and got dressed I could smell the aroma of breakfast trying to break my door down, and get to me, so I followed my nose to the kitchen.

"I'm surprised that you're the only one up," I said, taking a seat at the counter across from Aubrey.

"Well if the sounds I heard coming from Iree's room are any indication, then those two are definitely up. I'm not sure they've been asleep! Did you know?"

"About them having sex? Yeah, they connected when all that shit went down last year, and everybody was at our house in Mississippi. Girls will be girls," I replied.

"I'm not one to judge, I just wanted to make sure you were aware. Kyla and Dorian are awake too, she's in their room feeding him his bottle."

"They're gonna grow up thicker than thieves," I said, smiling at the thought.

"Mmm-hmm, just like me and Dollar. I remember that when we were little and my parents passed away he wouldn't let anyone near me. I mean he couldn't have been about nine or ten years old, and I was six, but he acted like my big brother and father wrapped in one. Whatever I needed, he got me. When I started my period at age twelve I went to Dollar, and he made sure that I knew how to use a tampon and a pad. When I lost my virginity at fourteen he put together a whole presentation on all the options there were for safe sex, and then he went and beat the teeth out of the mouth of the boy I'd slept with. When I asked him why, he said to make sure the nigga never spoke bad about me."

Hearing this made me laugh because it sounded exactly like the man I fell in love with. Protective didn't even begin to describe how Dollar was when it came to what he loved, which was why he tried his hardest not to love anyone. He didn't have a choice with me though because I'd made him love me before he knew what was happening.

"I'm surprised he didn't beat your ass before the safe sex talk Aubrey."

"Oh I'm sure that he wanted to, but he wanted me to learn from my mistakes so he knew that he had to let me make them. Trust me, it wasn't easy for him."

Even as I smiled at her my mind flashed back to how mad Dollar had been when I'd gone rogue, and went to visit my baby daddy in prison. The man that I met that day wasn't about to let me make my own mistakes, not if he could help it, but I wasn't mad at that. The way he'd handled me had actually made me love him more, and the sex was beyond anything that I'd experienced. When my eyes locked with Aubrey's I could still feel the smile on my face even as the sadness crept into my heart.

"I miss him too," she said, softly.

"Yeah, I know. I'm sorry."

"Sorry? What are you sorry for, it wasn't your fault that your own sister betrayed you and turned you in," she replied.

All I could do was nod because it was on the tip of my tongue to confess my sins about why I was truly sorry.

"Dorian stinks," Kyla announced, coming into the kitchen with his empty bottle.

This made Aubrey and I laugh because it was what Kyla always said when he needed his diaper changed. Kyla would do anything for her baby brother except change his shitty ass.

"I got it," I said, getting up and heading for his room.

As I neared Iree's door I heard a girlish giggle followed by a sensual moan, which made me tap on the door.

"Breakfast is almost done, and you two are required to eat more than each other so cut that shit out. And wash your hands!"

"We-we're cumming!" Iree yelled back, sounding like she meant it literally.

I shook my head, and continued on to Dorian's room where I found him half asleep with his big toe in his mouth.

"You really need to use your pacifier little man," I said, picking him up out of his crib.

His response was to show me his gums as he grinned up at me in a way that melted my heart.

"I love you too little Dollar," I said, covering his face with kisses.

I loved the sound of his laugh almost as much as I had his fathers, and so I kept him giggling the whole time I was changing him. The sudden sound of a plate shattering, followed by a loud thump, snapped my attention towards the kitchen and had me running for my room across the hall. I quickly grabbed my .45 from under my pillow, and went to put Dorian in his crib before I went to investigate. The sound of Kyla crying reached my ears as I got to Iree's door, and Iree must've heard it too because she stepped out with my four-barrel Glock.12 in her hand. With my left hand I motioned for her to go low as I went high when we turned the corner. Once she nodded her understanding we made our move quickly, ready to kill or be killed. What we saw when we sprang into the kitchen made us both drop our guns on the floor.

"Ohhh shit," I mumbled.

Chapter 8
Dollar

"What's wrong wife, you look like you've seen a ghost," I said, smiling lazily.

"D-dad, is it really you? Iree asked, moving towards me slowly.

When I opened my arms to her she hurried into them, and sobbed uncontrollably.

"Daddy! Daddy!" Kyla yelled, latching onto my leg and squeezing with all her might.

I wanted to pick her up, but there was no way to move around Iree at the moment.

"What's going on?" Rain asked, coming into the kitchen.

She took one look at Aubrey's unconscious body on the floor before looking at me, and running straight to me to occupy the other part of my chest that Iree didn't have. I'd mentally prepared for having to face Honey, but there was no way I could prepare for all the emotions that came with being reunited with my kids. The proof of this was in the fact that I could barely see because the tears were blurring my vision as they poured from my eyes. I held on tightly to the two little women sobbing in my arms, but I never stopped watching Honey. Part of me wanted to believe that she wanted to pick her gun back up to finish me off, but I knew she wouldn't do that with the kids right here. The complete and utter terror on her face said exactly how she was feeling.

"How-how dad?" Iree asked, gasping for breath while looking up at me.

"That's a long story sweetheart, and it's not important right now. All that matter is that I'm here, and alive."

She nodded her head, and went right back to sobbing uncontrollably. The sound of Aubrey stirring is what finally got Honey to move, as she went to her side and helped her up.

"Did I faint? I was cooking, and I thought Dollar was still alive because—"

"Because he is," Honey said, pointing at me.

For a second I thought Aubrey was about to go down again, but she held onto the counter and started praying as her own tears fell. My eyes swung back to Honey and I could see the emotions within her warring on her face, but she was still as beautiful as ever. I mouthed the words *I love you* to her, and that's when her resistance finally broke completely. The tears running from her eyes moved as fast as she did to my side where she stood on her tip toes so that she could give me a quick kiss. I felt the insatiable hunger for her ignite instantly, but before I could indulge she'd pulled back and hurried from the room.

"Up daddy, up," Kyla insisted, pulling on my leg.

Without having to be told, Iree and Rain took a step back so that I could pick Kyla up, and then they all somehow managed to hug me at the same time. We stayed huddled like that until Honey reappeared with a carrier in her hand.

"Would y-you like to meet your son?" she asked.

"A son? I-I have a son? We have a son?"

She put her hand over her mouth to stop the sob from escaping, but the tears still fell as she nodded her head and moved towards me. This time when Iree stepped back she took Kyla into her arms, and Rain stood by her side so that Honey could come to me.

"That's Dorian daddy," Kyla said pointing.

"Dorian?" I asked, looking at Honey.

She nodded again, while sitting the carrier on the counter and taking him out of it. When she handed him to me I held my breath, but the way he smiled at me as if he'd known me every day of his life melted me, and reduced me to tears again.

"He-he looks so much like me, but I see you too. He had your eyes," I said, looking directly at Honey.

I felt like I was staring at her soul, and with nothing more than a glimpse I could tell that she'd been through her own version of hell since she'd pulled that trigger on me. Knowing that made my heart ache for her, but I wasn't as surprised as I'd thought I'd be by that reaction. I knew that was because deep down I'd always known that my love for her was still there. I held my son close, kissing his soft skin while making sure that every sight, sound, and smell of this moment was imprinted on my brain forever more. Those were the moments that I'd been robbed of with Kyla, and to think that I had almost robbed myself this time made me mad. I wouldn't focus on that now though, now was the time for me to live in this moment because to not have it would've been this biggest regret of my life.

"Re-Re, I'm hungry," Kyla said.

Her innocent statement made everyone chuckle, and I could tell just at a glance that I'd interrupted breakfast.

"I'll take care of that while you girls set the table," Aubrey said.

Nobody wanted to move away from me, but I gave them a reassuring smile so that they knew I wouldn't vanish like smoke. As everyone started to move around I motioned for Honey to follow me outside into the bright morning sunlight. I kept Dorian in my arms, amazed that he was actually falling asleep right before my very eyes. I walked with him out on the patio and down towards the beach so that the conversation I was about to have wouldn't be overheard. The beauty of this moment was picturesque, but I had to introduce some ugliness into it in order to preserve that beauty.

"So are you happy I'm alive sweetheart?" I asked once she'd stopped beside me.

"I don't know how to answer that question."

"Try answering truthfully wife."

"You wanna talk to me about truth muthafucka?"

I didn't have to look at her to feel the full heat of her blazing stare, or to know how sexy she looked pissed off. I remembered both very well.

"To be honest, I didn't have a plan when it came to any conversation with you, so I'm not sure that the topics of truth and full disclosure are where I wanna start. Let's keep it simple. What did you tell them about the night I supposedly died?"

"I told them that you got caught in a gunfight, and you'd insisted that I go in front of you down the tunnel and not look back. When you and my dear sweet sister didn't make it out I naturally assumed the worse, and so we've all been morning."

"You have, huh?" I asked, looking over at her.

"Me not as much as everyone else, but I'm sure that you can fully understand why. Let me ask you a question though, how are you still alive?"

"You're not as good a shot as you think…unless you missed my heart on purpose," I replied.

"Your heart? What heart? If you had a fucking heart you wouldn't have been fucking my sister behind my back for god knows how long! That right there showed me that you were heartless because I gave you all of me in a way I'd never done for anybody else, and you shit on me! You shit on me for a bitch that shitted on you, and you did it with a smile on your goddamn face the whole time! So you don't have a heart Dollar, you're just a lucky motherfucka."

I could feel her body vibrating the air in between us, which told me that we were past anger and headed towards rage. Her raising her voice had startled Dorian awake, but I smiled at him and rocked him gently to keep him content in my arms. I knew that Honey had a right to feel the way that she was, even though I felt like her shooting me should've definitely made us even. I also knew that hollow excused or justifications would only escalate her anger, so I kept my mouth shut for a few moments to let her calm down.

"I'll make sure that my story forever matches yours so that they don't know what happened," I said.

"Gee thanks."

Her sarcasm was evident, but I simply laughed it off.

"I missed you Honey, I really did."

"Don't."

"Don't what?" I asked turning completely towards her so that I could verify the pain that I heard in her voice.

"Don't fucking act like you love me or miss me, or any of that bullshit because it's all a lie. You never loved me, and you know it."

"Didn't I though? I mean think about our entire relationship, and not just one moment in time. In your heart you know that I loved you because that love existed when

I thought that Katie was still dead. My love for you had been and always will be real, but if you need proof just look at this gorgeous little boy that we created. Honey he was created in love."

"Love doesn't lie Dameian, and no matter how you spin it that's still the truth. Maybe you did love me, but you obviously stopped feeling that way or you wouldn't have forsaken the vows that we took."

"You mean the vows that you and Malcolm Joyner took?" I asked.

"Oh, so the name difference means that you can fuck my sister?"

"That's not what I'm saying, what I'm saying is—"

"You know what, I don't give a damn about what you're saying because its bullshit and it don't matter no more. You're alive, she's dead, so now what? I hope you don't think that because you suddenly decided to rise from the dead that that means you and I stand a chance of getting back together, because it absolutely doesn't. I wouldn't let your dick near me if it was the last one on Earth."

The look of disgust on her face was so poignant that it pissed me off instantly, but I knew I had to remain calm because I had Dorian in my arms.

"First of all, I wasn't asking for us to get back together, nor was I offering to give you any dick. Secondly, you should really stop making assumptions about shit, or didn't anyone ever tell you that you'll only make an ass out of yourself when you do that?"

"What the fuck ever nigga, I know you, and I know that you didn't just pop up to say help. You think that you're gonna take me and those kids back—"

"Actually I only came for the kids," I stated calmly.

Beneath the anger in her eyes I saw the light of hurt flash on and off like a set of high beams, and that didn't sit well with me.

"Let me clarify my statement. After your activities in Amsterdam it became obvious to me that you're no longer putting our children's best interests first."

"How-how do you know about Amsterdam?" she asked slowly.

My response was a wink and a smile, which only served to infuriate her more.

"I taught you everything you know, and you did a good job, but I knew what to look for. The fact that you're out here in those streets putting in work unnecessarily as opposed to surviving in a life and death situation indicates that you've changed, and that change isn't good for the kids right now."

"Are you-are you calling me a bad mom?" she asked, narrowing her eyes as she stared up at me.

"No sweetheart, I'm saying that you're hurting and not thinking straight, and that will harm those that you love. If you don't believe me, or if you believe that you have everything under control, just stop for a moment and smell the air."

I could tell by her expression that she was confused by what I was saying, but when I looked over her head in the direction of the cottage that had recently burned down her expression changed.

"That was necessary because—"

"If you say it was, then it was. You should've got everybody off this island before you made your move, and you're smart enough to know that. So why didn't you do it?" I asked.

Her silence was all the answer that I needed, and I didn't say anything else because I wanted what I was saying to sink into her brain. She knew as well as I did that she absolutely could not afford to be reckless because there were too many people depending on her. When the tears started to fall from her eyes I could tell that she realized how bad shit could've gone, especially had I actually been dead. Less than fifteen minutes ago she was the center of the universe for all the kids in that house, and the very innocent baby in my arms, so every decision that she made had to be the right one. The weight of that responsibility had her tears falling faster.

"I-I'm sorry Dollar, I know you trusted me with their lives and-l."

"And I still trust you, but I'ma need you to move accordingly because I know that you know how," I said.

"You're right I do, so how do you wanna play this?"

"Well, I think Rain and Iree need to go back to Alabama immediately before the Feds get involved in a major way. Kyla can go to Louisiana, and you, me, and Dorian can be out of the country within a couple hours. You can pick the destination, I'll get you two settled, and then—"

"Wait, why is Kyla going to Louisiana? Who's gonna take care of her?" she asked.

In the back of my mind I'd been trying to figure out the most delicate way to say that Katie was still alive, but no words had materialized during our entire conversations. That left me no other option except brutality.

"Katie is in Louisiana, and she need Kyla because—"

"The fuck? That bitch is still alive too?"

Her explosion startled Dorian so bad that he started crying instantly, and me rocking him wasn't doing shit to calm him down.

"Honey stop yelling and just—"

"Fuck all that shit you're about to kick my way and tell me straight up. Is my sister still alive?"

"Yes Honey, but—"

"And you let her live, knowing that she snitched on me? You've actually been laying up with this bitch for the last ten goddamn months?" she raged.

"It wasn't like that, we were healing from being shot and—"

"Oh, so what you're saying is that you ain't been fucking her? You expect me to believe that bullshit Dameian?"

I opened my mouth to tell the lie that I knew she needed to hear, but before I could utter a word she mushed me in the face and stormed off back to the house. I felt like I could almost see the steam coming out of her ears because she was so mad, but this wasn't a laughing matter. For the sake of the little boy in my arms I had to make shit between me and his mother better, and aside from killing Katie I didn't have a clue where to start. I contemplated my next move while rocking Dorian back to sleep, and walking down towards the water. I was a man use to finding the solution to any problem, no matter how difficult, and part of that success was because I had no problem with killing whoever stood in my way. The problem now was that I was standing between two women that it would hurt me to kill. As a person who was determined to never love I now found myself in the middle of some shit that love had caused, and it wasn't going away. I paced back and forth slowly once I got to the water's edge, listening to the soft crash of the waves and my son's deep rhythmic breathing while trying to formulate a plan. After a while I finally had to acknowledge that the first step I needed to take was to talk to Honey, and so I made my way back towards the house. When I got to the patio door I had to quickly side step before Dorian and I got ran over.

"Careful Iree, you almost—"

"Cops-cops dad!" she panted breathlessly.

"Where?"

"Out-out front. They got Honey."

Hearing this made me quickly pass Dorian to Iree and instruct her to stay outside with him. When I walked in the house Kyla was sitting at the table waiting, and based on the sounds I was hearing everyone else was out front. When I got to the front door I saw Aubrey pulling a hysterical Rain into her arms as one of the four cops put handcuffs on Honey, and shoved her into the backseat of a cop car. Our eyes locked briefly, and the message in Honey's was clear. I didn't have to ask what happened because it really didn't matter when it came down to it. She was a fugitive, wanted dead or alive.

Chapter 9
Honey

I'd experienced heartbreak before in my lifetime, on multiple levels for multiple reasons, but none of that compared to the shattering I felt in my chest as I watched my daughter cry out for me. Out of all my kids Rain was the most like me, and that made my bond with her special on a different level, so to see her emotionally destroyed as I was handcuffed and put in the car was worse than anything I'd ever experienced. The look in Dollar's eyes told me that he understood the severity of this situation, but I didn't feel confident that I could count on him to save me this time. How could I fix my mouth to say that I needed him after what I'd done? I knew that I could rely on him to take care of all of our children, but that was as far as I would allow myself to believe in him. In this moment I felt more alone than I could ever remember being, and the reality of that forced the tears that I'd been fighting against to fall like midnight rain as we pulled off. I kept my head bowed and my eyes closed, until the car came to a stop, and my door was opened. I took a fortifying breath before climbing out of the backseat, and following the cops into the small police station.

"What's this?" a desk sergeant asked, from his seat behind the hole in the bulletproof glass surrounding the intake desk.

"Her alias is Felicia Abbott, but her real name is Tabitha Joyner. She's wanted by us for questioning in the Carlessio Pettycola homicide, and the great state of Tennessee wants her for capital murder. Two counts," the cop escorting ne explained.

This news was processed by the desk sergeant with a low whistle and a sad head shake.

"You're too beautiful to be doing all this killing miss Joyner."

"I ain't killed nobody, and I want a lawyer," I replied, calmly.

"You need to see the magistrate judge first," the desk sergeant said, pointing down the short hallway to my right.

I was steered in that direction and guided to another hole in the bulletproof glass. After a few minutes a cute black woman appeared, and informed me that my extradition to Tennessee would be happening sooner than later. The fact that the judge told me straight up that they didn't have enough to convict me of what happened to Carlessio worried me because it meant they wouldn't fight to keep me in their jurisdiction. I acknowledged that I understood, and then I was led into the back where my processing would begin. I was familiar enough with the fingerprint and mugshot procedure to not have to be told anything twice, which had all of it done quickly. A female cop searched me before taking me to a heavyset detective to be questioned.

"Mrs. Joyner, you were seen on the beach with Carlessio Pettycola the night before he died, so where did you two go once you left there?"

"I went to find my lawyer. Is he here now because I'd love to speak with him?"

My response actually made the detective chuckle as he wrote something down on the tablet in front of him. I expected some more back and forth because they needed a confession to make any crime stick, but instead I was dismissed, led to a single cell, and given a bag lunch. The tiny room had a toilet in the corner, and a cot with a flimsy mat that would kill a bitches back, but it smelled and looked clean. There was no way I could eat, so I laid down and tried to think of a way out of this shit. I thought I'd been careful about my approach when it came to Carlessio, especially considering that it was a private beach. I hadn't been careful enough though, and the community was small enough to spot an outsider anywhere. They couldn't prove a damn thing out here, but back in Tennessee was a different story. I closed my eyes and allowed my mind to travel back to the fateful day that now had me captive in a foreign jail cell. The knowledge that I'd been trying to save my sister's life made my stomach turn, because if I knew then what I know now I would've let that bitch bleed out. Better yet I would've double taped her hot ass, and left her brains on the motel room floor like dried semen. My feelings about Dollar being alive were mixed and confused, but I know exactly how I felt about Katie still drawing breath. If it was the last thing I did, I vowed that she would die before I did. I wanted desperately to be the one to permanently erase her existence from the Earth, but at this point I was ok with paying to get it done. The bottom line was that she had to die. She had to! I let that thought carry me into a restless sleep that was filled with nightmares. In my dreams I saw the most beautiful outdoor wedding, and I saw Dollar looking like new money in his black tuxedo. I saw Dorian too, looking like a miniature version of his dad, only he was about three or four years old, and he was the ring bearer. The scene was amazing, until the veil on the bride came up and I saw that it wasn't me. It was Katie. At this point I knew that I had to be dreaming, but I couldn't wake up! I was forced to watch the entire ceremony between my husband and the bitch that use to be my sister, and when it was over the unthinkable happened. The dream started all over again! I had no idea how long I fought this endless cycle of madness, but when my eyes finally opened to take in the jail cell around me I was drenched in sweat, and crying in a way that made it hard to breathe.

"It's okay sweetie, it's okay."

I looked to my right, surprised to find a nurse standing almost over top of me holding a washcloth in her hand. I tried to move away from her, but I couldn't go far because my hands were restrained to the bed by handcuffs.

"Wh-what the fuck is this?" I asked, feeling manic trying to overwhelm me.

"It was just a precaution because you've been thrashing around for hours. They wanted to give you a sedative, but I couldn't authorize that because I don't have your medical records."

"Don't give me any drugs! I'm-I'm fine, just let me go," I insisted.

"I can't let you go, you're under arrest and—"

"I know that, I just meant for you to uncuff me from this bed. I'm fine now, just let me up."

I could see the skepticism in her eyes as she stood there staring at me, but after a few moments she walked out of the cell. When she came back it was in the company of a tall black cop that I hadn't seen before.

"You've got a visitor Joyner," the nurse said.

I thought she was trying to be funny, but after the cop uncuffed me he motioned for me to follow him out of the cell. I was led down the hallway and through two doors before we came to a stop outside a room with a placard on the door that read attorney visits.

"You've got fifteen minutes," he said.

I started to argue because no law would ever allow for there to be a time limit on lawyer visits, but when he opened the door to the windowless room I saw who was actually here to see me. Without a word I stepped into the room, and once the door closed I hurried into Aubrey's arms.

"I'm so glad you're here," I said, crying softly.

"You should already know that you would never be left for dead."

Her statement gave me chills because I wondered if Dollar felt the same way, but I pushed that thought from my mind.

"How are my babies?" I asked, pulling back so that I could look at her.

The sadness was easy to spot, but I knew it would've been worse if Dollar wasn't around.

"Of course Kyla and Dorian are oblivious, but Rain and Iree are taking it hard.

It's beyond bittersweet for all of us because we're grateful that Dollar is alive, but nobody was prepared to lose you."

"I know. They don't got shit on me out here, it's the shit in Tennessee that's got me jammed up," I said, frustrated.

"I know, Dollar and I talked."

Hearing this had me looking at her warily, but I didn't say anything to give life to my secret.

"Did he tell you that my sister is still alive?"

"Yeah, he told me everything that's happened in the last ten months. They got extremely lucky that Savannah and Denise were staying in his other house because if not they would've surely died."

"I don't understand why he's let Katie live after what she did. Why Aubrey? I mean I thought he loved me, but for him to be still with her—"

"First of all, he does love you. I don't know what you mean by him being with her because from what he said they've been healing up, and trying to figure out what the next move was."

"So you really think that given their history they ain't been fucking?" I asked sarcastically.

"Absolutely not, and is that really what's been on your mind? Come on Honey, you know that Dollar loves you and he would never do no shit like that. He only tolerates Katie for Kyla's sake, and to answer your question, that's why he let her live. Trust me, I asked him the same damn question once he told me about his plans for the kids."

"You cannot let him give Kyla back to that bitch Aubrey, she doesn't deserve her and she'll only use Kyla to get to Dollar!"

"I don't have a choice in the matter, but I promise you that Dollar ain't going into this blindly. He's given me access to all the cameras on his property in Louisiana, and I'm supposed to watch everything until he gets there."

"Wait, he's not going back to Louisiana, is he?" I asked.

"Not right now. He's sending Kyla with Iree as her escort while he focuses on the more pressing business."

With the look she was giving me I didn't need to ask what business he found pressing, but I didn't allow myself to get excited. At this point I didn't know whether to consider my husband a friend or a foe, but I was leaning towards the later.

"So when are you all leaving?" I asked.

"The jet had already been charted because Dollar wanted to get Rain out of here before word travelled that she was actually here. I had to come see you first because there's no telling when I'll be able to sit down with you again."

The tears clouding her eyes and slowly cascading down her cheeks spoke to how close we'd gotten in this last year, and I knew that she understood what I was feeling without words being spoken. I hugged her again tightly, and put my lips directly on her right ear.

"Protect Dorian with your life Aubrey. You're his godmother, and you promised to always do for him what I couldn't. I'm expecting you to keep that promise now."

She pulled back and looked at me for a second before gently kissing my lips.

"On my life I will keep that promise, and look after him as if he were my own. You never have to worry about that."

"Thanks sis," I said, taking a step back before turning towards the door.

"Do you want me to tell Dollar anything?" she asked.

I paused and thought about what she was asking. There was so much that I wanted to say but knowing that he'd been sleeping with the enemy made it all seem insignificant.

"Tell him that I owe him one."

When I glanced over my shoulder I could see the puzzled expression on her face, but I didn't bother explaining before I tapped on the door and it was opened for me. I followed the tall cop back to my cell, and a few minutes later the nurse returned with a cup in her hand.

"I brought you something to help you sleep peacefully."

"I told you that I'm not taking no drugs, so thanks, but no thanks," I replied, laying down and facing the wall.

She took the hint and left me alone with my thoughts. An hour later I was wishing for those sleeping pills because I couldn't shut my mind off, but the last thing that I needed was to put anything in my system that would allow my body to crave. I needed a completely clear head for what was coming next. I had a lot of thoughts to sift through in terms of what defense best suited me, but somehow my thoughts always went back to Dollar. Before I knew it, the sun had set and risen again, and the only thing I'd accomplished was putting together a Dollar highlight reel of events in my mind! I desperately wanted to stop thinking about him, and when my breakfast was brought to me I was given that chance in a major way.

"Joyner, breakfast! When you're done put these on so that you can go," a female cop said.

"Go where?"

Looking at the orange two-piece jumpsuit she was holding out gave me an idea, and bad feeling about what she meant.

"The U.S. Marshals are here to take you home to Tennessee."

Chapter 10
Dollar
Tennessee
Two weeks later

"Alright listen up. The goal today is the same as any other day, which means we want to have a nice and peaceful shift. Headquarters in Nashville is paying attention to this facility in particular because of the Fentanyl overdoses from a few weeks ago, so be mindful of that. Do your security checks on time, and make sure that your logbook is updated accordingly. Are there any questions?"

Not one hand was raised, and a few moments later Captain Higdon dismissed the shift change meeting.

"Gates, you're with me today," Sgt. Olasin said, motioning for me to follow him.

I rose from my seat and put on my utility belt, trying to appear nonchalant despite my excitement. For the past couple weeks, I'd been learning the layout of Bledsoe County correctional complex as one of their newest C.O.'s in training, but they'd been keeping me on the men's side of the prison. Today would be my first excursion over to the females side, which meant that I would finally get to lay eyes on Honey again. When she was arrested in St. Croix I'd thought that she would be housed in the county jail like most people awaiting trial, but somehow the prosecutor had gotten the judge to agree that she was a serious flight risk. Nobody knew, where her husband was, but her being Mrs. Malcolm Joyner meant that she was a woman of means, so they'd justified holding her in prison and adding a probation violation to her case so that she couldn't get bond. I knew that her frustration had to be ten times what mine was, and that could lead her to do some dumb shit, so I'd wasted no time getting myself a job as a C.O. Lemarcus Gates to the rescue! I didn't have a firm plan in my mind of how the fuck I was gonna get her out of this situation, but I felt like if I was near her then I'd be better prepared to seize any opportunities that came along.

"Alright Gates, today is gonna be a little different for you, but if you listen to me and follow my lead you'll be fine," Olasin said.

"Yes sir."

Understanding that I was now in the part of Tennessee where the Klan still roamed freely let me know that I was gonna have to kiss the ass of these good ole boys in order to accomplish anything without suspicion. It made my stomach turn, but there was nothing that I wouldn't do for Honey.

"So, what made you decide to be a C.O.?" Olasin asked.

"Well, I figured that this job is just as important as protecting and serving on the streets or in the military, but it's often not given enough credit. I mean the work that you all do is invaluable because if there's no one around to make sure the prisoners stay locked up then the world will fall into anarchy."

"Exactly son! I'm glad that you get it because so many people don't!"

I could tell by the smile on his face and his tone of voice that he was excited to have someone around who "Got it", and who felt like he felt. Honestly, I thought C.O.'s were certified babysitters, but I'd done enough research on the people working here to be able to speak their language. My ability to blend in would be the difference between success and failure.

"So how long have you been working in corrections?" I asked.

"A little more than five years now, but I just transferred to this prison about eighteen months ago. It's better than the last shit hole I worked at."

"How so?" I asked, following him out of the watch commanders office.

He waited until we were outside and headed towards the building where the women were housed before responding.

"Well, for starters the chicks here look way better, and they understand the benefits of giving a little to get a lot."

"I see," I replied.

"No you don't, but if you stick with me you just might," he said, winking as he slapped me on the back.

I had to fight against my natural instincts to knock some sense into his six foot, one hundred eighty-pound ass for having the nerve to touch me, but I managed to keep cool. We entered the building and went straight to his office. I did my part as the observer by watching him push papers for the first hour of our shift, while listening to him make calls around the prison compound to catch up on the latest gossip. Just from his side of the conversation I learned that there was a chlamydia outbreak amongst a few C.O.'s and some nurses because everybody was fucking everybody, and condoms were obviously optional. I wasn't here to judge anyone though, so I simply chuckled in the right places and filed the information in the back of my brain.

"Well, it's time to make a round in the trenches," he answered, standing up and stretching.

I wanted to scream the word finally, but I kept my eagerness low key and followed his lead. When we entered the first of three pods the smell of fish hit me in the face hard enough to make my stomach roll, and it took everything in me not to visibly gag.

"You'll get used to it," Olasin said, looking at me and laughing.

"Sarge, I need to speak to you."

The person who made this statement was standing in front of a bunk bed a few feet away from us, and my first thought was that he was out of place because men weren't allowed on the female side.

"What is it, Erika?" Olasin asked.

"I go by Maleah now Sarge, and the problem is that I missed my hair appointment because I was in medical."

It wasn't until the female walked over to us that I realized that she was actually a woman. She looked like a whole nigga, and the afro she was rocking wasn't helping to convince anyone that she had a vagina. I'd seen plenty of prison shows, so I knew this three hundred-pound, black critter was what they called a bull-dyke. I could tell just by the way that she looked at me that her dick was bigger than mine!

"Well Ericka, you know that I can't do anything about what day shift fucked up on," Olasin stated.

"I know that, but you can make sure my name is added to tomorrow's list before the master pass list printed out."

"And why would I do that?" he asked smiling.

They shared a look that didn't require words, but it only lasted briefly because Erika walked away. We continued on into the pod, moving through the bunks that were set up so that the pod functioned as a dormitory! The routine questions about commissary and toilet paper were asked, but for the most part the females just sized up the "new guy". I wasn't a fan of the kind of scrutiny I was getting, but I took it in stride. I'd thought that men were the only sex that would stare with a certain amount of blatant hunger until I'd made my first round in a female prison pod. The way almost every women locked eyes with me before looking down at my zipper and licking her lips made me feel like a piece of meat, and that was a completely foreign experience. By the time we'd made it back to the front door Erika was standing there waiting on us. Her hands were quick as she slipped a piece of paper into Olasin's hand, so I doubted anyone besides me saw her. Once we were back in the hallway he opened the paper, read it, and passed it to me to read.

"That's how things work around here. We call it a favor for a favor," he said.

On the slip of paper were four people's names, and Erika had wrote down who was selling dope, using dope, and holding the dope. The fact that I recognized my wife's name made me want to go punch that snitching bitch in the mouth, but I gave no outward reaction as I handed the paper back to Olasin.

"So now what?" I asked.

"Well, I'll probably have three of these bitches watched and searched, but as for the other one, I'll handle that personally. Come on."

I didn't know what he had in mind, but the predatory look in his eyes was hard to mistake for anything other than what it was. When we got to the door of the second pod, he motioned for the C.O. manning this post to come out into the hallway.

"Send Dewitt out here," Olasin demanded.

The C.O. nodded and disappeared. I know that my bored expression hadn't changed, but inside my blood was heating up in my veins, and the familiar feelings that came with being in Honey's presence were coming over me. My mind understood how important it was to stay in character, but my heart was beating fiercely with the want to take my sweet Honey away from here. I made a conscious effort to breathe in and out slowly to calm myself, and by the time she stepped out in the hallway I was under control. She only glanced at me briefly before turning her attention on Olasin, but I couldn't take my eyes off of her. I could tell that she didn't have any panties on under the loose-fitting gray shorts, and the bra she had on beneath her V-neck t-shirt had her titties sitting up like she was eighteen years old. The way her long hair curled up at the ends told me that it was wet, and her fresh face appeal meant that she had just got out of the shower. She looked good enough to eat, and I could tell Olasin was thinking the same thing.

"Sergeant Olasin I ain't done nothing, so why are you calling me out here?" Honey asked.

"Dewitt I always check on you when I come down here because you and I go back a long ways, but tonight isn't just a social call."

"What's that supposed to mean?" she asked, glancing at me again.

"Well sweetie, your name was brought to my attention as someone who is selling dope in here, and after that girl overdosed a couple weeks ago we've been told to crack down on all drug activity."

"I ain't been doing a muthafuckin thing, so whoever told you that is a bitch ass lie. I just got back in here, so you know I ain't had time to do anything or be a part of anything Olasin."

"I know that, and I can probably convince the warden that you're not doing anything when the time come. If…"

"If what? If I'm willing to suck your dick?" she asked boldly.

He chuckled at what she said, but I didn't find a damn thing funny. I tried to defuse the situation by coughing into my hand, but when I did that Honey looked at me in a way that was unsettling. I didn't know exactly what thought had crossed her mind, but I know her well enough to know that it wasn't good.

"You want me to suck your dick Sergeant Olasin?" she asked softly, with a slight smile.

"I never said that Tabitha, you did."

"But you've said it before though, right? As a matter of fact, didn't you tell me that if I gave you some of this good pussy that you would be my connect for anything I needed while I'm here."

When Olasin glanced at me I could immediately tell that he was wishing that I was anywhere except standing here with him. I didn't doubt a word coming out of Honey's mouth, but his look confirmed her words anyway.

"Tabitha, I don't recall that conversation, but—"

"Sure you do, but you don't want to admit it with the rookie right here. He looks like he can keep a secret though, so it's okay to speak your truth. You can keep a secret can't you C.O. Gates?" she asked, making a show of looking at my name tag.

Her tone may have sounded friendly to the sergeant, but I could hear the accusations in her voice and I could see the anger in her beautiful eyes. Both of those things gave me a bad feeling.

"Even god keeps secrets," I replied.

"That's cute Gates, but we're not talking about god right now. Right now we're discussing a secret between the three of us because the sergeant here has wanted some of my good pussy and head for years now, and today just might be his lucky day," she said.

"Really?" Olasin asked quickly.

The smile on Honey's face didn't reach her eyes, but Olasin was too blinded by the prospect to notice. The sudden feeling of rage shooting through my body made me colder than a winter night in Canada, but I kept my expression completely neutral.

"Does your offer still stand, Olasin? Will you be my plug and take care of me while I'm here?" she asked.

"Absolutely."

"How do I know that I can trust you once I've given you what you want?" she asked.

"As a show of good faith I'll tell you who just told on you, and I'll give you the list of informants in this building," he replied, passing her the piece of paper that Erika had handed him not long ago.

"Erika, huh? I always knew that sloppy built bitch wasn't shit."

Honey tucked the slip of paper down in between her titties, and then she stared at me for a long moment. Olasin had no way of knowing that we were communicating, but we were and it was ugly I could read her mind like I'd pulled the top off of her pretty little head and took a peek, and what she was thinking could be summed up in one word. death.

"There's one condition to this, Olasin. If I let you fuck me then the rookie has to be in the room to watch."

"That's fine, so let's—"

"No," I stated calmly.

"What did you say Gates?" he asked, looking at me.

"I said no, I'm not watching you two."

"It's just like watching porn, Gates, only better," Honey said, smiling devilishly.

"Nah, I'm good, you two have fun with that and—"

"If he doesn't watch then the deal is off Olasin, so you better talk to him," she said, staring at me pointedly.

"Gates if you want this job then you'll follow me, and keep your fucking mouth shut," Olasin said, taking Honey by the arm and leading her away.

I reluctantly followed them to a door at the end of the hall where Olasin struggled to find the right key to unlock it and let us in. He ushered us inside what appeared to be a counselors office, and quickly shut the door behind us.

"We gotta make this quick ok, I don't know what time the lieutenant is gonna make his rounds," Olasin said, hurriedly unbuckling his utility belt and pulling it off.

Honey and I stared at each other across the room, and I could see the defiance blazing in her eyes.

"Trust me Olasin, you won't last long in this good pussy," she said, never taking her eyes off of me.

"Don't," I said in warning.

I knew that she knew that fire that she was playing with, but I didn't understand why she was taking this risk. My presence alone should've let her know that I was here to help her, and that I'd somewhat forgiven her for shooting me, but the look in her eyes said that she didn't want my forgiveness. She wanted to hurt me.

"Take your shorts off," Olasin demanded, unzipping his pants and pushing them down.

"You got a condom because I'm not about to get pregnant."

When he held up the bright red package with the Trojan logo on it Honey took it from his hands and tore it open. Even as she pulled the condom out and rolled it down his dick, she kept her eyes locked on mine. He was standing in between us with his back to me, which meant that I could've snapped his neck and ended this game, but I stood right where I was. I needed to know how far she was gonna take this because that would decide our future.

"I want you to fuck me hard," Honey said.

She let her shorts drop to her ankles, and she stepped out of them before sitting on top of the desk behind her.

"I'ma fuck you good and hard," Olasin said huskily.

Without hesitation he stepped in between her open legs and shoved his dick inside her hard enough to snatch her breath away. For a brief minute my vision swam and I couldn't see, and then all I could see was Honey's toned legs wrapped around Olasin's waist as he fucked her fast. There was a smile on her face as she stared at me, but the look in her eyes was hollow. I couldn't explain the emotions shooting through my body, but since I knew that I couldn't control them I just completely shut down. When I did that the screaming in my mind suddenly faded, and over the sounds of Olasin grunting with each stroke I heard a door close inside me. When that door closed I smiled at Honey, and I'm not sure what she saw in my expression, but hers turned to panic quickly.

"W-wait, Olasin. Stop, please stop," she said, pushing against him.

"Al-almost done," he panted, fucking her faster and harder.

"No, no stop! Stop!" I could hear the edge of hysteria enter her tone, but it must not have reached Olasin's ears because he kept pumping away until his body finally shuddered mightly. When he backed up she hopped off the desk, and hurriedly pulled her shorts back on, but now she wouldn't look at me.

"Relax Tabitha, the condom didn't break and I'm a man of my word. Besides, your pussy is as good as you said it was, so I'm definitely gonna bring you whatever you want to keep this thing going. Gates, do you wanna get a quick ride in?" he asked, turning to face me as he fixed his clothes.

"Nah boss, that's all you. She's not my type anyway."

My comment made Honey look at me, and I could see the pain that the anger had been masking.

"Not your type? What are you talking about, she's beautiful. I'm telling you that the pussy is amazing too," Olasin insisted.

"Beautiful, huh? Ask her how beautiful she feels right now."

I could tell that she was fighting hard against the tears, but she lost that battle and they poured from her eyes like a sink overflowing.

"Whoa, we don't need all that damn crying Tabitha. Get your shit together, and officer Gates will escort you back to your pod," Olasin said, fastening his belt.

He made a quick exit, which left Honey and I alone.

"Dollar, I—"

"My name-is Officer Gates," I stated slowly.

"Baby please, I just—"

I ignored her words and walked out of the office.

"Dollar! Dollar, talk to me! Dollar, I'm-I'm sorry please!

I didn't turn back or pause in my stride, I simply wiped my tears away and kept walking. By the time my shift ended I understood what door I'd heard close in my mind. It was a coffin. Honey's coffin.

Chapter 11
Honey
3 days later

"Hey, Tabitha, are you okay?" Lacy whispered, squatting down next to my bed.

"N-no," I replied, continuing to sob softly into my pillow.

I'd been in the same position on my bed, curled up crying until I was so exhausted that I had to sleep, for the past three days. I hadn't washed my ass, ate, or moved other than to throw up and lay back down so that I could cry some more. I didn't know ninety-five percent of the bitches I was locked up with so I didn't feel like I owed them any kind of explanation, but Lacy and I had done time together before. I had told her what happened, but she knew me well enough to know that I wasn't devastated like this for no reason.

"What is it sweetie? You know that you can talk to me," she whispered.

I looked at her with every intention of giving her a pretty lie, but the ugliness of the truth reduced me to sobbing all over again. I didn't resist when she pushed me over closer to the wall so that she could climb her five-foot six inch, one hundred fifty-pound self in the bed with me, and I willingly went into her arms when she wrapped herself around me. Her actions soothed me in a way the words couldn't, and I just cried like I'd never cried before.

"It's okay Tab, whatever it is will be okay."

"No, it-it won't, Lacy. I've lost him for good this time."

"Who sweetie? Who did you lose?" she asked.

More tears poured out of me before the answer could, but once I could finally speak I ran the whole situation down to her. Even though I trusted Lacy, I still gave her highlights for most of my history with Dollar just because I needed to keep parts of him sacred and to myself. The one question that I'd been asking myself since I'd felt Olasin's dick inside me was, "how did I fuck this up so badly?"

True enough Dollar had broken my heart, and he deserved to answer for that, but how did me fucking a man in front of him make him do anything more than hate me? I knew that he hadn't fucked Katie with the intentions of hurting me, but I'd absolutely fucked Olasin for that purpose. Even knowing that he'd literally come to prison to save me, I'd still did that foul ass shit. Why? The pain that was inside me that I'd used to justify my actions had disappeared quicker than Olasin's climax, especially when I'd seen the change in Dollar's eyes. Up until the point that Olasin had penetrated me I'd enjoyed watching Dollar's emotions war inside him, I'd enjoyed his pain and discomfort. I'd thought that that was what I wanted, but the moment I saw him disconnect from his emotions I knew in my soul that I had been wrong. Now I had no idea how to undo what I'd done, and my biggest fear was that it couldn't be undone. I'd truly lost my soulmate.

"Damn girl. I mean I understand your pain, anger, and thirst for revenge, but..."

Lacy didn't have to finish her thought because the continuous shattering in my chest said it all.

"He-he won't even l-listen to me Lacy. I know I fucked up, but so did he!"

"True enough, but you obviously didn't forgive him, so do you really expect him to forgive you with this still fresh in his mind?" she asked softly. The answer to that question only forced me to cry harder. When Lacy squeezed me tighter I took advantage of the security she provided and cried myself to sleep. I didn't know how long I stayed asleep, but I awake alone in my bed with the weight of sadness pressing on my chest mercilessly. I laid there for a few moments until my brain registered that what had woke me up was the sound of everyone leaving the pod to go to dinner. I waited until there were only a few stragglers left climbing from my bed, grabbing my shower stuff, and heading for the bathroom. While taking my time brushing my teeth to erase the sour taste of tears and vomit I contemplated the quickest way to commit a painless suicide. It wasn't until I looked in the mirror and saw the innocent smiling face of Dorian looking back at me that I was able to snap out of it. I may have sincerely wanted to die, I couldn't take the cowards way out, which meant that I had to pull my shit together. I took my time under the tepid waters spray while the beat built in my mind until there was a loud mantra screaming one thing at me. I had to get out. I knew that there was absolutely no counting on Dollar at this point, but he'd proven that he wouldn't expose me to Aubrey, which meant I still had one powerful ally. I took care of my hygiene and dressed quickly, and then went in search of a spot in the line for one of the three phones that inmates could use. It wasn't until I'd actually gotten in line that I noticed the small groups of females huddled together whispering. This behavior only added up to something happening, and I could tell the whatever it was had to be major.

"What's up Melissa?" I asked, tapping the short blond chick in line in front of me.

"You ain't heard girl? Sgt. Olasin's entire family was slaughtered. I mean they were completely butchered, even his kids were chopped into pieces! It's been all over every news station late last night."

"Do the police know what happened?" I asked genuinely concerned.

"That's the crazy part, there's absolutely no trace of anyone at their house, which is where all of this happened."

To me that wasn't the crazy part, that was all the confirmation I needed that Dollar was behind this. My brain was trying to caution my heart about reading too deeply into what Dollar's actions meant, but my heart was already beating harder with hope. Would he really do all of that if he didn't still love me, or was this simply wishful thinking? I let this question rotate on my satellite as the line for the phone inched forward. By the time I had a receiver in my hand, I knew who I had to call first.

"Hey sis, it's me," I said, once Aubrey answered.

"It's about time that you called bitch because now you can tell me what happened."

"What do you mean?" I asked, cautiously.

"I mean what the fuck happened between you and my brother?"

The way she phrased this question sent feelings of panic from my spine to my stomach, and back again. The faith that I'd had about Dollar keeping my secrets from Aubrey was immediately shaken, but I decided to proceed with caution before simply telling on myself.

"What did he say, Aubrey?"

"Nothing, and that's my damn point! I know Dollar better than he knows his damn self, so I know something is wrong, and your three day silence tells me that it has everything to do with you. Especially given current events, so spill the beans bitch."

Despite how close Aubrey and I had become I knew instinctively that the truth was off the table for sure. So what was I gonna say?

"I don't know Aubrey because I ain't talked to him."

"You haven't? well he told me that he saw you a few days ago, and the next thing I know..."

The way that her statement trailed off told me that I was gonna have to give her some type of explanation because saying I didn't know wasn't holding up.

"You know how possessive Dollar can be," I stated simply.

Silence hummed over the line for a few seconds, but I could hear Aubrey thinking loudly that I was hiding something.

"How's Dorian?" I asked, changing subjects.

"He's fine, but I can tell that he misses you. We all miss you."

"I miss you all too. When was the last time you spoke to Rain and Iree?" I asked.

"You know that I talk to them every single day, and I've got eyes on them too. Rain finally went back to school, and we pulled a few strings to get Iree in the same school with her because they insisted on being together. Right now Iree is in Louisiana with Kyla though I doubted that my bitch ass sister would hurt her own child. I put nothing past Katie at this point in life because she'd proven how grimy she was, but I would most definitely have the last laugh.

"I'm surprised Dollar actually left Iree and Katie under the same roof," I said.

"He only did it so that he could deal with your situation. Hearing this only caused more guilt to weigh me down, but I did my best to shake it off and focus on the purpose of my call.

"How is everything looking Aubrey?"

"Honestly…I'm worried. For obvious reasons I'm not gonna say too much, but let's just say that the great state of Tennessee has convicted mufuckas with less evidence. I don't have to remind you that they still impose the death penalty out there, especially for capital crimes."

No, she didn't have to remind me. I'd faced a jury of twelve out here before behind witnessing a murder that I'd refused to speak about, and they'd tried to burn me then. If I didn't beat this I was dead, and it was that simple.

"What's Dollar saying?" I asked.

"At first you know what he was saying, but something changed and now I honestly don't know where his head is at."

"Aubrey you can't let him leave me. I know that he probably doesn't love me, but for the sake of my son you've gotta talk to him," I said, fighting the tears I could feel in my throat.

"Honey what happened?" she asked, gently yet forcefully.

"I-I fucked up."

That was really all I could say before the salty taste of fresh tears filled my mouth, forcing me to turn my back on the pod so that I wouldn't be seen crying again. Thankfully Aubrey didn't push the issue, although I could hear the exasperation in the deep breath she took before speaking.

"I got you sis, but you need to fix whatever you did to fuck up, and stop fucking up. You've been given a miracle, and I don't have to explain how, so don't take even one moment for granted. You hear me?"

"Yeah, I hear you loud and clear, and I love you more than I can say. Do me a favor and kiss my little man for me, and tell him that his mommy loves him more than life."

"I will. Make sure you stay strong mentally, and keep your eyes open. I love you and see you soon." She said, disconnecting our call.

My heart still hurt as I hung up, but my hope remained steadfast. The sound of a familiar voice caused me to hang up the phone slowly and turn around even slower as a feeling of dread filled me with a quickness.

"That's right, you bitches know what it is so you better keep your girl out of my sight because its cuffing season," Erika said, cackling as she pushed a cart with her property on it into the pod.

Just when I thought my life was about to get back on track it took a turn in the opposite direction. I immediately felt my blood boil as our eyes locked, and this flat nasty bitch had the nerve to smile at me like shit was sweet.

"I know that look Tabitha, and she ain't worth it," Lacy said, coming up beside me.

Despite my instant fury, I was about to agree with Lacy until I spotted Dollar coming through the door behind this bald head bitch, carrying some of her shit.

"Is that—"

"Yeah, that's my husband," I whispered through gritted teeth.

"He's cute."

"Not now Lacy," I said, locking eyes with him.

I was trying to read his expression and his mind, but he wasn't giving shit away. The fact that he was here at all spoke some positivity to the animal in me that I was trying to keep quiet, but him being with her still didn't sit right with me. I kept quiet though, and simply observed. Erika stopped a few beds away from mine and began to unpack her stuff. To everyone's amazement, and my displeasure, Dollar's helpful ass was assisting her like she was some type of damsel in distress. Every second he spent with her made me grit my teeth that much more until my jaw was aching, and throbbing.

"Come on Tab, let's go outside," Lacy suggested.

"Nah, I'm good."

"You know that he's just doing this to get under your skin Tab, but he obviously still loves you."

I didn't respond to her statement in any way, I just kept watching Erika laugh and joke with my nigga. When she actually walked up on him and started whispering to him, I'd officially had enough.

"C.O. Gates, can I speak to you?" I asked, heading in their direction.

"When I'm done," Erika replied sweetly.

"I wasn't talking to you bitch," I growled.

"Tab, chill," Lacy said.

"Yeah, chill and stop cockblockin because he don't want you bitch. As a matter of fact I doubt anyone wants you now that you let Olasin fuck you," Erika said, laughing.

She hadn't raised her voice, but she'd definitely spoken loud enough for others to overhear, and that was evident by the loud gasps that I heard around me.

"Only a weak bitch would spread lies about a dead man," I replied.

"Rumors? I don't spread rumors, I only speak facts. Ain't that right C.O. Gates?"

I fully expected Dollar to defend my honor and silence this warthog built bitch, but instead he just chuckled and shook his head. That hurt more than her words, but I refused to let them see me sweat.

"Oh, so you're looking for the cops to be your witness now? Damn bitch, I guess being on their payroll comes with all types of perks, huh?" I asked sarcastically.

"Snitchin bitch," Lacy said loudly.

"Lacy if I was a snitch I'd be speaking on whose dick you were sucking yesterday, so shut that shit down how. As for you Tabitha, you're funny and its cute that you tried to switch the subject away from your dirty deeds. I get it though, you're ashamed that you got ran through by a nigga that the ugliest bitches have turned down cold. You know what, just throw your pussy away because its officially trash now."

"On my worse day I'm still twice the woman you are bitch, and my pussy is way better. Why don't you ask C.O. Gates that," I replied, closing the distance between us with a few quick steps.

"How would Gates know when he refused to fuck you after Olasin finished."

Erika's statement stopped me cold in my tracks and forced me to look Dollar in the eyes because there was only one way she's had those details. The blank look on his face made my heart hurt more than anything, but I did my best not to let it show. It was obvious that he was on some serious fuck shit, but I held onto the hope that it would make some type of sick sense.

"You better check the source of your info sweetie because nobody turns down this good pussy, and a square nigga like Gates would marry a bitch like me," I said, smiling.

The sound of Erika's laughter made my blood boil, but I didn't let it show outwardly.

"Marry you? Damn bitch, you really are delusional, huh? Personally I think he'd marry Lacy first."

"Shut the fuck up Erika," Lacy said quickly.

"Why Lacy? You wouldn't like the idea of marrying C.O. Gates in the real world?"

Erika's question sounded innocent, but something about the smirk on Dollar's face gave me a feeling of extreme unease. When I looked to my right and saw the barely masked horror on Lacy's face my heart slid into my stomach.

"What's up, Lacy?" I asked.

"Tab, I swear that I didn't know," she replied immediately.

Right then I know whose dick she'd sucked yesterday.

Chapter 12
Dollar

The look on Honey's face told me that pieces of this ever-expanding puzzle were sliding into place still, but I knew that she didn't see the big picture yet.

"So y-you sucked his dick Lacy? Damn, you didn't waste a second did you?" Honey asked, shaking her head.

To the others it was probably easy to see her anger, but I saw through that to her pain. Last week that might've moved me, but her moment with Olasin had made sure that I couldn't feel shit except for disgust for her.

"Tab, I didn't know who he was and—"

"What does it matter Lacy, you act like you owe that bitch an explanation or something. I was just pointing out that sweet Tabitha would be the last bitch Gates chooses. Shit, I got to this dick right after you did!" Erika said, snickering.

Hearing this made Honey's head snap around to me quickly, and I saw the rage blazing brightly in her eyes.

"You fucked with this bitch knowing that she snitched on me? So, it wasn't enough that you did that shit with my sister, you gotta fuck with these nasty bitches that I can't avoid being around?"

"Wait, you fucked her sister too?" Erika asked, laughing loudly.

I could feel the fury of murder literally vibrating off of Honey, and I know she was on the edge which meant she only needed a little more nudging.

"Lacy, I need your help real quick. It's your job to re-fill the chemical bottle's right?" I asked, completely ignoring both Honey's question and the look she was giving me.

"Y-yeah, but I-."

"No but's, let's go. Maleah I'll see you before shift change," I said, winking at Erika.

Before Honey could utter another word I slipped her a sealed plain white envelope, and walked away. I could see the hesitation written all over Lacy's face, but I took ahold of her arm and steered her towards the front door of the pod before she could say anything else. We went to the closet where the supplies were located, and only once we were inside where no one could hear us did we speak.

"Are you who Tabitha says you are?" she asked immediately.

"Who did she say I was?"

"Her husband who she just hurt by fucking someone in front of you."

"Would that have changed you wanting to swallow my cum?" I asked seriously.

She didn't say anything, but the way she glanced down at my dick said it all.

"It's obvious that you love her or you wouldn't still be here, but I don't get why you're trying to provoke her. You do know that she's fucking crazy, right?"

"Love don't got shit to do with this right now, I'm simply here for the sake of my son needing his mom. As for provoking her, don't worry I know exactly what I'm doing because I absolutely know the woman that I married. It's okay though, she won't hurt you because she's about to have some fun with Erika."

"So you do have a plan?" she asked, nodding her head.

"Yes I do, and right now your part of this plan is to either suck my dick again or get fucked. Which would you prefer?"

"Wh-what? I can't do that now that I know who you are. Tab is my friend."

Her voice held the right amount of sincerity, but the slight sweat on her brow said more than her words. A quick glance at my watch told me that we had less than five minutes before shit got serious, so I decided to skip to the part that made Lacy's decision for her. I softly unzipped my pants, pulled my dick out, and just stared at her. The internal war on her face was comical because she still ended up looking down at my dick like it was her last meal on Earth.

"Why is this my part of the plan?" she asked softly.

"Because you're Tabitha's friend, and I owe her for what she did. I mean I could've chose someone else, but she's close to you, plus you're sexy. Your head game is average, but what you lack in skill you make up for with enthusiasm."

"Average? My head game is average?"

It was easy to tell by her tone of voice and the way that she asked this question that she was offended. My response was to look pointedly at my watch while lightly massaging my dick with my right hand.

"Let's see how long you last this time," she said seductively, taking my dick in her hands and squeezing it purposefully.

It didn't take more than five seconds for me to be rock hard, but instead of taking me into her mouth she quickly pushed her pants and panties to the floor, and turned her back to me. When she slowly bent over I got a beautiful view of her almost hairless pussy along with her juicy ass.

"Pick a hole, and fuck me like you mean it," she demanded huskily.

I wasted no time inching up behind her, pushing my dick right up against her pussy lips, and shoving inside her swiftly.

The heat and tightness reminded me of Honey, and that made me plow into her harder. I grabbed her harder. I grabbed her by both hips to prevent her from falling or running, and I dove deeper until I could feel my balls slapping against her rhythmically.

"Uh-huh damn daddy! Fuck me harder," she stammered while squeezing my dick with her pussy walls.

My strokes became more intense, but the sudden squawk of the radio on my hip froze me in mid stroke.

"Help needed in twenty-eight C pod! Assault in progress! Weapon visible! All available C.O.'s report!"

"Is-is that Tab?" Lacy asked breathlessly.

"Yeah, so we gotta go."

Even as I said those words I was back pumping away inside of her, loving how the wetness of her pussy echoed off the walls around us. I could hear footsteps in the distance heading in our direction, but I knew that they wouldn't make it to us because the pod was three doors up from the closet. I grabbed a handful of her brown hair, and let her juicy ass bounce off of my thighs as I pounded us both into a quick orgasm. Before her body could stop shuddering I'd pulled my dick out of her, and wiped it across her big ass.

"Allow me," she said, turning around to face me.

She quickly put her heart shaped lips to work by slurping all the juices off my dick and balls, causing my vision to swim with the aftershocks from my climax.

"Stay here until the coast is clear, understand?"

"Yes daddy," she purred, looking up at me submissively.

I hurriedly straightened my clothes, put my dick away, and slid out of the closet. I blended in with the other C.O.'s rushing to the pod and pulled up a good distance away from Honey like everyone else. I could hear several C.O.'s and sergeants pleading with Honey to stop, but she was ignoring them while sitting on Erika's chest, and cutting her over and over again. Erika's screams were little more than gurgles at this point thanks to the huge gash in her throat, but Honey kept right on slicing her face and neck with the razor in her grip. The look in her eyes was reminiscent of our time spent with Father Brennan in Chicago, meaning that it wasn't safe for anyone to approach. It was time for me to make my next move. I pushed my way to the front of the crowd, and eased up beside Honey. Ignoring the warnings of my co-workers and superiors, I leaned down until I was close enough to whisper to her without being overheard.

"That's enough Honey. Now I need you to get off of her and hand me the razor."

My soft spoken words caused her to pause in midswing and stare at me. For a few seconds I could tell that she was looking straight through me, but the sudden return of the rage to her eyes let me know when she was actually seeing me.

"Don't do anything stupid Tabitha. If you try to kill me right here you're gonna force me to kill you, and I'll get away with it. Not to mention, you'll fuck up my plan to get you back to Dorian. Stay focused on your son and not who I've fucked," I advised firmly. ˈ

In the back of my mind I knew that she wanted to slit my throat and let me bleed out, just like I knew she could smell the fresh sex on me now.

"You did this Domeian, and it's not over. It's just the beginning."

"Be that as it may, I need you to give me that blade so that we can get out of here," I replied, holding my hand out.

There was a moment's hesitation before she dropped the bloody blade in my palm, but once she did everything happened at once. Honey barely had time to get off of Erika's body before a dog pile of C.O.'s hopped on her ass and rode her to the ground roughly. Despite the knees in her back and the hands mushing her face into the ground Honey didn't utter one word. The nurses appeared within seconds, but one look at Erika and everyone knew that she was long gone.

"I don't know how you did that Gates. But I appreciate you defusing the situation before it got worse. You've got a bright future in this field," Lt. Starks said.

I turned towards the short, attractive red bone, admiring her curves that I knew gave way to a phat ass dragging behind her.

"Thank you Lt. I was just doing what came natural," I replied.

"Oh, so dealing with hostile women comes naturally for you, huh? Well hopefully your personal life is easier to manage."

The look in her eyes was definitely a flirtatious one, and my smile let her know that I was interested.

"So what happens now?" I asked.

"Well since a weapon was involved, and the victim is dead, the prisoner will be transported to the nearest police station to be officially charged."

"And who does the transport?" I asked curiously.

"Well normally it would be whoever is on transportation, but given how well you handled the situation I think that you should take part in it."

I made a show of looking around to make sure that the lieutenant was talking to me before I spoke again.

"I mean if that's what you want me to do, I don't mind working overtime. Just tell me what to do."

"First, I need you to make sure you tag and bag that weapon properly, so why don't you come with me," she replied, leading the way through the thinning crowd.

I spared Honey one more glance before following Lt. Starks switching hips out of this pod. Once we got in the hallway I spotted Lacy making her way towards us slowly, and I nodded discreetly at her so that she would know everything was good. Lacy gave me a slight smile, and after that my focus was on the Lt. with the big booty. I knew she'd be the supervisor today, just like I knew that she'd had her eyes on me since our first encounter when I'd started my training cycle. In truth, I knew more about her than she thought I did, but she'd be pleasantly surprised soon enough. She led the way out of the building housing the female dorms to the main building where her office was located. When I walked into her office my nose was immediately filled with the sweet, yet subtle, scent of her perfume and I wondered if her entire body smelled as good.

"Okay so I'm gonna walk you through the proper procedure for chain of custody and—"

"Actually Lt. that's not even necessary because I'll be taking the razor with me," I stated.

"Yes you will, but the local authorities like things done a certain way before we turn evidence over to them."

"Oh, you misunderstood me. What I mean is that I'll be taking it with me when I leave so that it no longer exists for anyone to use against Tabitha," I said calmly.

The look of confusion on the Lieutenants face didn't take away from her beauty, but it didn't match her expression.

"Gates what are you talking about?" she asked.

I took a seat across from her desk, and contemplated my words.

"Okay Latoya I want you to listen to me carefully so that I don't have to repeat myself. I think now is a good time for you to call home. Your mother Jackie won't answer, but if you call your brother Kameron he'll be able to explain a little of what's going on. Make sure that you use your cell phone because your work calls are monitored by this institution."

The disbelief was clear to see in her brown eyes, but it vanished quickly as the smile on my face widened. With shaky hands she fumbled in her pocket until she found her phone, only taking her eyes off of me long enough to punch in the necessary numbers. Her call was answered after the first ring, and she never got the chance to say hello before the beam of panic sounding baritone came over the line. I couldn't make out the words that Kameron was speaking to her, but I didn't have to guess because I knew what she was being told. Judging by the slight quiver of her succulent full lips, and the sudden loss of color to her face, I knew she was learning about the two pounds of C4 that were strapped to her kids backs. The fact that they were sitting at home in the safety of their own living room watching cartoons wasn't about to make the lieutenant feel any better, so I didn't offer that hollow platitude

"All you have to do is follow directions, and this thing will have a happy ending. If you don't, you'll never find all the pieces to put your kids back together," I stated calmly.

Every ounce of flirtation and playfulness had vanished, but the blatant horror that replaced it was in some ways sexier to me. It fed the demons lurking inside in a way that nothing else could.

"Wh-what do I have t-to do?" she asked shakily.

"You'll do whatever I say, now hang up the phone."

Chapter 13
Honey

"D-Dewitt, step up to the door and cuff up."
I recognized the voice giving the command as that of Lt. Starks, and that only further irritated me. Normally I didn't have a problem with her, but I'd heard her flirting with Dollar while her minions were pinning me to the ground. Right about now her thirsty ass could get it just like that big bitch Erika had.
"Cuff up for what?" I asked, not moving from my position on my new bunk.
Aside from having my sweet revenge on Erika's snitchin ass I also get the benefit of having my own cell now, which meant alone time with my thoughts. That was worth his weight in gold after living in a dorm full of funky, moody, trifling ass women.
"You gotta go before the magistrate in Bledsoe County."
Her response didn't truly surprise me because I'd felt Erika's soul leave her body two minutes into our bloody dance, but I'd kept cutting her in hopes of releasing all the rage that I felt. I'd had no idea what Dollar was slipping into my palm after the way he'd played me in front of everyone, but discovering the razor made me smile genuinely. I had no idea what his entire plan was, I just knew that killing Erika gave me some momentary satisfaction. Hearing that I was about to be formally charged with another murder dampened my mood a little, but it was still worth it.
"Are you gonna feed me first?" I asked, scooting off the bed and making my way to the door.

In response the tray slot was dropped, and all I heard was the sound of handcuffs being opened. I backed up to the door and allowed her to cuff me before stepping to the side so that the door could be unlocked, and opened. I turned around expecting to see Lt. Starks, but instead I came face to face with Dollar. There was so much that I wanted to say, but I didn't utter a word because I was evaluating the situation rapidly. The bored expression on Dollar's face was one I'd seen before, and it matched perfectly with the twinkle of mischief in his eyes. One look at Lt. Starks and I could tell that she was a deep breath away from vomiting, which meant that whatever play Dollar had put down was surely epic by definition.

"Lt. Sparks, you look like you need a long vacation," I said, chuckling softly.

"She'll get one with all expenses paid if this goes right," Dollar said.

His comment had only been loud enough for the three of us to hear, but the sound of his voice still caused Starks to visibly twitch, she was shook.

"Lead the way," I said, smirking.

Lt. Starks spun on her heels and headed up the hallway, which left Dollar with the task of taking me by the arm and following her.

"So, this was your plan, husband, fuck bitches until it drove me crazy enough to kill."

"Genius, right? I got the idea from you," he replied emotionlessly.

I had some smart shit on the tip of my tongue, but I knew there was no point in antagonizing him. At least not, until my freedom was secured. I was wondering just how difficult it was gonna be to get me out considering that we were headed to a more secure location, but I knew that I had to trust Dollar. We followed Lt. Starks out of the side door of the building where an idling transport van was waiting. Dollar put me in the back, Starks got behind the wheel, and then he got in the passenger seat.

"These-these vans have built-in GPS," she said, looking over at him.

"I know that Latoya, so just drive to the police station and I'll let you know what happens next."

It took us about five minutes to clear the prison's grounds, and when we did I breathed a sigh of relief while vowing to never come back. It was a quick twenty minutes later when I could see the jail looming in the distance, and that's when Dollar started giving directions. Instead of going to the garage door that would've took us to the sally port, Lt. Starks pulled up in the parking lot next to an all-black Chevy suburban.

"I want you to get out and move like it's natural for us to be switching vehicles with a prisoner," he said.

"But I—"

"No buts, just remain calm and this will all be over shortly," he said, opening the door and climbing out.

He quickly pulled me out of the van and pushed me into the back of the Suburban before going around to the driver's side. Starks was moving with obvious hesitation, but I could tell by Dollar's movements that he wasn't worried about whether or not she'd plant her ass cheeks in the passenger seat. Within a couple minutes we were loaded up, and on the move again. Dollar drove at a normal rate of speed until we excited the city limits, and then he put the pedal to the floor. Before I knew it we'd made it to the city of Crossville, and we were pulling up in front of a townhouse.

"Take all of the restraints off of her," Dollar demanded.

Starks climbed into the backseat with me and quickly did as she was told, while tears streamed silently down her face. The look of dejection in her eyes told me that she knew that death was more than likely around the next corner, and she was trying to make peace with it. When the last restraint was removed she reluctantly climbed back into the front seat, and waited.

"If I don't kill you, then they'll look you up because they'll say it's an inside job," Dollar said softly.

If I didn't know any better I would've sworn that I heard real regret in his voice, but I knew that was impossible. Dameian Morgan didn't feel regret or remorse, all he felt was that the ends justified the means. Hearing his words and truly understanding their meaning made Starks cry harder.

"My-my kids, pl-please they're only—"

"Honey look under my seat and grab the leather bag," Dollar said, ignoring her.

I reached blindly under the seat until I felt what he described, and then I passed it to him. He didn't even open it, he simply tossed it in Starks' lap.

"Open it," he said.

Her hands were shaking so badly that I was tempted to smack her in hopes of snapping her out of it, but I played the background. When she finally got the bag open she just stared at the contents like she'd never seen anything like it before.

"I-I don't understand," she stammered.

"It's simple, Latoya. I'm letting you and your kids leave. That's two hundred fifty thousand dollars you're holding in your lap, completely untraceable and tax free. I could easily kill you, your kids and your family, but instead I'm choosing to buy your life. That means as long as any of you are breathing, you owe me. Understand?"

"I-I understand. What do you want me to do?" she asked, wiping her tears away.

"We're gonna go inside and set the scene really quick, and once we're safely away, I'll call the bomb squad," he replied.

"Bomb squad?" I blurted out.

He gave me a brief glance before turning back to Starks.

"Ok. I swear I'll never say a word to anyone about either of you!"

"Oh, I know you won't, and it's your job to make sure that your family doesn't either. I will kill every last one of you, and I'll do it with a smile on my face. Understand?" he asked, smiling widely.

Once she nodded her head, Dollar opened his door and got out, leaving us to follow his lead. We made our way inside the house where a man and woman sat on a couch side by side, each of them sporting a bulky vest full of C-4. I was about to ask why the woman had tape on her mouth when no one else did, but the fire in her eyes told me that she had a lot to say. Dollar quickly secured Starks to the little boy and girl sitting on the floor in front of the T.V, making sure that each of her arms were tied to one of her children. When that was done, we left as quietly as we'd come, after stashing the money in the back of Starks' closet and erasing all evidence of our existence. Once we were alone in the Suburban with the open road in front of us, and night falling all around us, the awkward tension built. Dollar turning on the radio was a blatant play at eliminating the need for conversation, but I knew there was too much to say.

"Where are we going?" I asked.

Judging by his outward appearance one might think that he hadn't heard me over the sounds of Rick Ross rapping, but I knew better.

"I asked you a question Dameian," I said, turning the radio back off.

"Does it matter where you're going as long as it's not back to prison?"

"Yes, it matters, because I wanna see my kids. Plus, we're not about to waste this opportunity to clear the air about everything, so you might as well start talking."

"There ain't shit I need to say," he replied calmly.

If I didn't know him I would've believed him, but I did know him.

"Oh, so you don't wanna talk about you fucking around with them trifling ass bitches in there?"

"No more than you wanna talk about you fucking Sgt. Olasin, and making yourself one of them trifling ass bitches," he replied, pressing down harder on the gas pedal.

The pain I felt in my chest couldn't be covered by the anger pumping through my veins at the thought of what he did with Erika or Lacy. As badly as I wanted to carve a pound of flesh out of his body for having the audacity to sit next to me smelling freshly fucked, I could still see the look in his eyes after I'd fucked Olasin. I knew that I'd hurt him, and I wanted to move past that, but how could we if we didn't talk?

"Look, I know that I did some foul ass shit, and I'm not about to sit here and try to justify it. Truth be told, no matter how many of the bitches you fucked it still doesn't make us even because what I did was worse. You came to save me and I let my hatred for Katie blind me to the love you have for me. I'm so sorry, Dollar."

"Had for you."

"Huh? I replied, confused.

"The love that I had for you, as in past tense."

"Dollar, I know that I fucked up, but I also know that you still love me, because it doesn't go away that quickly. I still love you despite all that you've done."

"That's the difference between you and I, Tabitha. I honestly don't love you, and I suggest that you don't confuse what I just did with love that you think I have for you. I did this because of my love for Dorian, and the rest of the innocent lives that were affected by you being locked up. None of that was about us, and that's why I fucked them other bitches. Think about it my darling wife, and tell me what logical reason I have to be sitting next to you with Lacy's scent all over me aside from the fact that I wanted to fuck her."

His words were like a knife to the heart, but I turned my face towards the window so that he couldn't see how hurt I was. The truth was undeniable, and it was crushing my heart, but part of me knew that I deserved it. This time when he turned the radio back on I didn't reach to turn it off, or turn the volume down. Instead, I tried to focus on how I was gonna lock my feelings away because it was clear that there was no changing his mind. That didn't mean that I was giving up or conceding defeat, but I knew all too well how stubborn Dollar could be. As the miles flew past, the hurt in my heart changed to hope as the faces of my children took up space in my mind. I couldn't wait to see them, hold them, and simply be in their pres-ence. Thinking about how devasted Rain had been when they'd put me in the back of the cop car had haunted me, and even caused silent tears to leak from my eyes now. I'd never wanted any of my kids to witness what Rain had, and the fact that she did made me feel like a complete failure. I couldn't change what happened, but I'd rather die than let it happen again. I didn't know what the future held, but it was becoming painfully obvious to me that I needed to plan my immediate future without Dollar in it as my husband. I laid my head against the window and let that thought carry me into subconsciousness, but I awoke before I could start drooling when the SUV came to a stop. I opened my eyes and looked out of the windshield at the hulking figure of Dekalb County Hospital.

"Alabama is the first place they'll look for me, Dollar. I can't stay here."

"Don't act like I'm stupid Tabitha, just get out of the truck," he said, opening his door and climbing out.

I followed him across the parking lot to an all-black old school '67 Camaro and got in the passenger side. When we got back on the highway I made sure to pay attention to all road signs until I had some idea of where we were going.

"Are you seriously taking me to Louisiana, like I won't kill my fucking sister?" I asked in disbelief.

"That's exactly what I'm doing because I'm sure you won't kill Kyla's mom in front of her. Besides, all we're going to do is pick the kids up, and get out of the country before the heat from the hunt for us becomes unbearable. So, for the sake of the children that you claim to love I'ma need you to keep shit cute."

I could already feel the hole in my tongue from biting it because I had a lot I wanted to say, but none of it would help the widening gap between Dollar and I. So I remained silent, and went back to sleep. When I awoke again the moon was high in the sky and we were gliding to a stop in front of what could only be described as a mansion.

"Oh, this is very inconspicuous," I said, sarcastically.

"You damn sure didn't know we were here."

"Fuck you, Dollar, because—"

"No thank you," he said, leaving me in the car to argue with myself.

I got out, and was on his heels quickly.

"Let's get something straight husband, you're not about to be an obnoxious asshole to me forever, so go ahead and get it out of your system. You know that it's not good for the kids to see or hear you be so cruel to me."

I knew that I was close enough for him to hear me, but he kept the same purposeful strides while ignoring me. I had every intention on arguing until he agreed to my point as we came through the front door, but a familiar smell scattered my thoughts. The way Dollar stopped in his tracks and pulled his gun out told me that he definitely smelled what I did.

" Could it be an animal?" I whispered.

"No, that's definitely a human that's dead."

I stayed close to him as he inched further into the house, knowing that we'd more than likely find Katie's body around any corner. I wouldn't act like I was disappointed, but I did hope that Iree hadn't done it in front of Kyla. The sound of a strangled scream made the hair on the back of my neck stand up, until I realized where it came from. I'd never heard a sound like that come from Dollar. Before I could say anything I saw him slump to his knees, and I heard his gun drop to the hardwood floor.

The sight of Iree laying on the living room floor in a pool of dried blood with a gash in her throat forced me to my knees beside him. The screams I heard now were louder, but they were different because they were mine.

Chapter 14
Dollar

I'd seen death almost as many times as God himself, and more than enough had been at my own hands, but this was different. Despite the certainty in my heart and in my mind that it was too late to save her, I still found myself crawling to Iree, and trying desperately to revive her. As I pressed my lips to hers and tried to breathe life into her I felt the coldness of her skin reverberate to my heart. I could hear my name being called from somewhere far off, but I ignored it because all I wanted to hear was Iree's voice. I just wanted her to say some smart shit about my breath stinking, or how she still owed me a bullet for that time I'd shot her. Deep down I knew all of that was impossible though. My baby was gone.

"I'm sorry sweetie," I whispered through the tears in my throat.

I lost track of time sitting there holding her so I had no idea how long Tabitha had her hand on my shoulder, but as soon as I noticed it I shook it off.

"If I hadn't had to rescue your dumb ass she'd still be alive," I said coldly.

I don't have to look back at her to know that she wanted to say something, and I know that if she did I was gonna lay her body right next to Iree's. I wisely felt her take a step backwards. It took me a few more minutes to pull myself together enough to stand up with Iree in my arms and lay her on the couch. I kissed her forehead before turning on my heels, and walking from the room. My destination was my office down the hall, and strides were purposeful. I went straight to my laptop, logged in, and pulled up all the security footage for the last forty-eight hours. The fact that everything had been wiped clean didn't surprise me, but I didn't panic because nothing was ever truly gone. Within five minutes I was looking at Iree's last hours, and what I saw put the taste of death on my tongue.

"You bitch," I growled through clenched teeth.

"Katie did this?"

My eyes flickered away from the computers screen long enough to lock eyes with Tabitha, who was standing across from me, and then I refocused on the screen. I didn't object when she moved to stand beside me so that she could see it with her own eyes because I knew how much she loved Iree. I wanted to be selfish with my loss, but I knew Iree would chastise me for that if she was still here. I took a couple deep breaths and suppressed the raging emotions inside me so that I could evaluate the footage properly, and then I replayed it. What I saw was an argument that turned into a fist fight, and after Iree whooped Katie's ass, she snuck up on her and slit her throat. Following that I saw the sheer terror and panic come over Katie, which made her next decision for her. She packed up her and Kyla hurriedly, and she ran. After reviewing the footage three times straight, watching my baby girl bleed out and take her last breaths alone, I pulled out my phone and dialed a number.

"It's me."

"Everything go as expected, bruh?" Aubrey asked.

"No. Iree-Iree is dead."

The hollowness of these words echoed in my ears, and even though I'd seen exactly how it happened it was still hard to believe.

"Dead? Wh-what? How?" Aubrey asked.

"Katie did it. Find her," I demanded, hanging up.

"I'm sorry Dollar, you know how much I loved Iree, and you know that I'll help you to hunt that bitch down. I don't care where we have to go," Tabitha said.

This time when she put her hand on my shoulder I didn't shake it off. Truthfully at this point Tabitha's presence was the only thing keeping me rooted to reality because I desperately wanted to just let go and lose it. The images on the screen blurred as more tears slid soundlessly down my cheeks, and to make it worse all I saw when I looked around my office were memories from the last time I was here.

"Take off your clothes," I said, suddenly standing up.

"What?"

Instead of repeating myself I grabbed her shirt by the collar and pulled it as hard as I could. Within seconds, her shirt was in tatters at her feet, and I was roughly tugging at her pants.

"Dollar, wait—"

My swift backhand smack forced her to swallow her words as blood sprang from her bottom lip instantly. The only thing that stopped her from falling or flying into the wall was the tight grip I still had on her pants. I pushed them down over her hips, and she wisely stepped out of one pants leg. In one motion I ripped her panties off, spun her around, and pushed her up against the wall while pulling my dick out. I shoved my way inside her savagely, quickly pinning her arms to the wall with her palms pressed flat against it like she was assuming the position. My second stroke was harder than the first, and the third ripped her pussy open.

"F-f-fuck!" she cried out.

I set the pace to break a bitch's neck, and I lost myself in the merciless pounding I was delivering. The taste of salty tears in my mouth only made me fuck her harder, and the smell of fresh blood from her pussy fed the animalistic rage in me. When I felt the surprise gush of her orgasm bathe my dick in her juices I pulled it out of her pussy, and shoved it in her ass. By stroke number two I was greeted with that same tearing feeling, and the sounds of pleasurable pain echoing off the walls. I spun her around and slammed her whole upper body on my desk, grabbed a fist full of hair, and kept right on fucking her. Every stroke was one of hate, and I enjoyed it as such.

I h-hate you bitch!" I growled, pumping faster.

"I-I know!"

Moments later I came with blinding force, and collapsed to the floor where I cried in sobbing gasps until I had no tears left. The feeling of my heart hammering in my chest was the only thing that let me know I was still alive, and I cursed it. I didn't wanna be alive right now, I wanted to give my life so that Iree could come back because she deserved to live. I didn't. That's all that I kept saying in my mind as the tears continued their endless run down my cheeks. When the dry heaves started I fought desperately to regain my composure, and not hyperventilate. It took a while for me to get myself together, but eventually I was able to climb off the floor. Tabitha was sitting in the chair behind my desk with her arms over her chest, staring off into space with unseeing eyes. Her pants were still around her ankles but seeing her naked didn't have the same effect as times past. Despite the fact that I'd fucked her and cum, I still couldn't stomach looking at her or sharing this space. Without a word I turned around and left her sitting right there. I went upstairs, turned the shower on, and let the water pound me. As the steam rose so did the wall around my heart, so that by the time I got out of the shower and got dressed I was completely numb. My focus now was centered on one thing, murdering Katie in the most painful way I could imagine. When I made it back downstairs to my office I found it empty, which was just how I wanted it. I wasted no time logging onto my encrypted email in hopes that Aubrey had picked up on Katie's trail. I wasn't disappointed in fact, I was surprised by how quickly Aubrey had narrowed her location. I picked up my phone off the desk and called her, just to make sure that I was reading her timeline correctly.

"It's me. Did this bitch really go to where I think she did?" I asked.

"Yeah, she's definitely in Florida, and I think she's looking for her dad."

I could see the logic in Katie's move because she didn't know her dad was dead, or that I'd been the one to kill him. I'd let her dad tell her that story though once I sent her to the other side.

"Ok, well I'll be loaded up and headed in that direction within the hour," I said.

"What about Honey?"

The way that she suddenly appeared in the doorway was almost like Aubrey mentioning her name had conjured her. The look in her light golden eyes was one of determination, and for some reason that annoyed the fuck out of me.

"I'll call you back and let you know," I replied, disconnecting the call.

"Did Aubrey find her yet?"

"You need to get ready to leave the country. Aubrey and the kids are on a yacht anchored off the Italian coast, which is for enough away for the moment," I stated.

"I'm not going anywhere except for after that bitch. Iree was important to me, and I loved her, so I will avenge her."

The forcefulness of her statement was almost convincing, but it was hard for me to believe a word out of Tabitha's mouth. Going to the extent that she had in the Virgin Islands for Iree spoke volumes, but I still knew that I could trust nothing about Tabitha.

"Don't you think that you need to comfort Rain while you still have time? Losing you will be hard, but learning that Iree is gone will surely devastate her in a way that only you can understand," I said.

"It's low for you to play me like that Dameian. I understand that Rain will be devastated, but nobody has to tell her right now. I think it'll go a long way towards the healing process if Rain knows that the person responsible for Iree's death had been dealt with. Plus if we tell her now she'll undoubtedly try to get involved with the search. After all, she is my daughter."

I hated the logic she came with because I knew the truth of it. Rain's impulsiveness was what had led me to her mom, so there was no doubt that she would go rogue because of her love for Iree. The only way to protect her from herself, and keep her out of the way, was to keep her in the dark for now.

"You're right," I admitted, begrudgingly.

"Wow, how did that taste going down?"

"Fuck you Tabitha!"

"I'm ready if you are. I mean, my pussy and ass are a little sore, but I've had both busted open before so I can handle it. You're welcome to take your frustrations out on this good pussy."

"Nah, I'm good. You served your purpose in the moment, but make no mistake I really don't fuck with you," I stated seriously.

I could tell that she had a reply on the tip of her tongue, but my phone ringing silenced her.

"What's up, Aubrey?" I asked, answering.

"She's gone off the grid, and I don't know where she's at."

I didn't have to ask who she was talking about, so hearing this only made my rage resurface instantly.

"I'm putting you on speaker phone so that Honey can hear you. Say that again," I replied, pressing a button on my phone.

"I said that Katie has gone off grid with Kyla. She could still be in Florida, and that's where I'm actively searching for her, but as of right now I just don't know."

I watched Tabitha absorb this information in silence, but her expression wasn't the mask of anger and frustration that I'd expected.

"You know where she's at," I stated, watching her closely.

Her eyes flickered up to mine so that she was staring directly at me.

"I may know where she's going."

"Aubrey, we're on the way," I said.

Chapter 15
Honey
Two days later
Florida

"I'm gonna be honest with you, Sebastian, if I were you I'd tell us everything that we wanna know because if not your imminent death will be the least of your worries," I said, licking my vanilla ice cream cone.

"I-I've told you every-everything I know. Please!"

The sight of a big strong man being reduced to tears always amused me, and now was no exception. It had been pure entertainment to watch Dollar strap Sebastian to a dolly, and pull both his fingernails and toe nails off with pliers. The melodic sounds of his screams echoed off of the walls of the abandoned warehouse that we were in like a Luther Vandross serenade. While it was true that he was nothing more than a lowly gardener, he was a gardener for my sperm donors widow. That meant that he could see behind the wizards curtain, and tell us if Katie was holed up in a mansion in Fort Lauderdale.

"You ain't told us shit yet Sebastian, and that's starting to piss me off!" Dollar said, throwing a short jab with his right hand.

The punch landing caused Sebastian's head to snap back viciously as blood instantly flew from his mouth, and coated his teeth. In the past forty-eight hours Dollar had killed three people employed by Anthony's widow, and their immediate family, so it was clear to me that he was not fucking around. I'd seen him handle business before, but the way he took his time butchering the ten people recently added to his body count let me know this was personal. I'd actually questioned Dollar's sanity when he'd gouged out a woman's eyes, and forced her husband to eat them or watch his infant son die from being cooked in their oven. This war path was one of biblical proportion, but so far it had yielded very little in the way of information about Katie. I felt like she would go to Anthony's widow because she'd had suck a good report with him before his disappearance. The survival instinct inside Katie would convince her that she could hide behind a lot of money, but truthfully there was nowhere she could hide. We were coming. I stood up from the chair I'd been occupying and used my free hand to pull the Glock 9mm from the small of my back.

"I'm bored," I stated, leveling the pistol at Sebastian's terrified face. I knew that he was opening his mouth to beg, but I let their well-placed bullets speak for me.

"I wasn't done questioning him."

"I know, but do you honestly think that you hadn't gotten everything possible out of him? I mean we know that Anthony's widow is here in Fort Lauderdale, and that her niece is staying with her. We don't know what this niece looks like, but I think it's a safe bet that it's Katie," I said.

"But he didn't say anything about Kyla!"

"Come on Dollar, Katie may be dumb, but she ain't stupid enough to just have your daughter out in the open. That's the first person that you'd look for."

I had no idea why he was suddenly looking at me with a weird expression on his face, and a twinkle in his eyes, but it was unsettling. I watched closely as he pulled out his phone and quickly dialed a number.

"Aubrey, it's me. Listen, I want you to put out an Amber Alert for Kyla, and make it known that she was spotted in the Fort Lauderdale, Florida area," he instructed.

Hearing this made me smile as I licked my ice cream. I couldn't hear Aubrey's response, but he disconnected the call with a smile on his face.

"What did Aubrey say?"

"Just that it was a great idea, and that she was on top of it," he replied.

I felt like there was more said, but I let it go. I tucked my gun away, and finished off my ice cream while he made the dead body disappear into the shadows of the warehouse. When he came back I led the way outside into the humid night air, got into the passenger side of the Rolls Royce Wraith. Once he was behind the wheel and we were on the move I carefully broached the next subject.

"So I'm thinking that after we send Katie to hell that you should come with me to Italy because the kids need you as much as they do me."

"Don't do that Tabitha."

"Do what? And I've told you before about calling me by my fucking government name."

"Calling you Honey is me being fake because I don't fuck with you like that. And you know what I'm talking about when it comes to your suggestion, so don't try to use those kids to play me."

"Ain't nobody trying to play you, Dameian, I'm simply pointing out that your kids would benefit from a two-parent household. Do you really want Dorian to grow up as another angry black man, or worse yet, Kyla became another black girl lost? The answer to both of those questions is no, so I think we need to at least consider all of us being under the same roof. Besides, if I'm ever caught you know that our kids are gonna need you."

My sales pitch was met with silence, but I could tell by the set of his jaw that he was contemplating what I'd said. The problem was that he was a stubborn muthafucka, and I'd wounded his pride with my dumbass actions.

"Look, Dollar, I've admitted numerous times over the past two days that I fucked up royally, and I sincerely apologize for it. So tell me what you need me to do to make this right because at this point I'll do anything you say."

"Anything, huh? Well then put your gun in your mouth, and pull the fucking trigger," he replied coldly.

In my heart I knew that he didn't mean what he was saying, but that still hurt beyond words. For a moment all I could do was stare at his profile, refusing to believe that the love of my life could ever truly hate me that much. When he didn't say anything else or acknowledge the heat coming from my stare I decided to find out. I pulled my gun out, chambered a round, and popped the clip out.

"You want me to kill myself, husband?"

He didn't verbally respond, but he did glance over at me briefly. I waited until we came to a stop at a traffic light before calling his bluff.

"If that's what you truly want from me, I'll do it because I love you that much, but you better have the balls to watch," I said.

He turned sideways in his seat, giving me his undivided attention, and crossed his arms over his chest. I wasted no time putting the gun to my head, making sure to lock eyes with him so that I knew he could see my soul. I could see the barely containable rage in his stare, with just a hint of disgust sprinkled in too. It may have been wishful thinking on my part, but I also thought that I saw traces of the love I knew he was fighting against, and that's what I held onto. My grip on the pistol was tight, but steady, and I felt no fear as I gently began to squeeze the trigger. It only took one time firing a gun to know exactly how much pressure needed to be applied before it went off, so I knew the point of no return. I was betting that he knew too since he was the one who'd given me the gun.

"I love you Dollar," I said genuinely, still applying pressure to the triggers.

He didn't reply except to yawn loudly, but I saw his eyes flicker away from mine long enough to examine the trigger. Part of me wanted to smile, but I didn't because I knew that I hadn't won yet. I could feel the sweat on my palms seeping into the rubber, which almost made it necessary to readjust my grip. I stayed the course though, squeezing the triggers steadily while praying silently. I didn't really wanna die, but the truth was that without Dollar part of me was already dead, and I couldn't live like that. I wouldn't live like we had been. When he still didn't move I understood what I had to do, and I accepted my fate. I gave him a sad smile before letting my eyes fall closed, and pulling the trigger all the way. The sound of the gun going off was deafening in the close confines of the car, and the sound of the passenger side window blowing out was equally as loud. It took me a few seconds to realize what had happened, and I opened my eyes.

"Why did you hit my arm?" I asked.

"Because you—"

The sudden sound of sirens stopped his sentence cold, and the flashing lights flickering across his face made my question pointless. I looked out the back window and felt my stomach seize at the sight of a cop car sitting right behind us at the stop light. Before I could ask Dollar what the plan was there were two cops standing behind their squad doors, with their guns out and levelled in our direction. That kinda made our decision an easy one. Without hesitation I popped the clip back into my gun, chambered a round, levelled it at the cops, and blew shots at them through the back window. I'd wisely taken aim at the driver first, and his head exploded with my second shot. I'd thought this would give Dollar time to make a fast getaway, but instead he threw the car in reverse, turned the wheel clockwise slightly, and stomped on the gas. It was obvious that this took the cop by surprise too because he never took the chance to get out of the way before we smashed him in between his door.

"I'm sorry Officer, I didn't see you there. Just hang tight and I'll help you," Dollar said, raising his own gun. The comical part in all of this was the fact that Dollar actually took his time to wind down the window before shooting the cop four times in the face. After that he put the car in drive and pulled off like everything was normal.

"We still make a good team," I said smiling harder.

One thing I knew about my husband was how much he loved killing, and not even his anger at me could steak that joy. We rode on in companionable silence back to the safe house we'd chosen as our base of operations for the moment.

"Are you hungry?" I asked, following him inside.

"Not really."

"Well will you let me cook for you anyway, just to do some normal shit for once?" I asked, hopeful.

"So killing cops ain't normal for us?"

"Touché husband, but you know what I'm saying. I just want—"

"How did everything go?" Rose asked, coming into the living room.

"Nothing we couldn't handle," Dollar replied.

Witnessing Dollar and Rose interact in the last couple days had made me uneasy, so it definitely didn't escape my mind that my loaded fun was still in my hand. I knew that I had to stay focused on the task at hand though.

"So are you any closer to finding Katie and your daughter?" Rose asked.

"Something like that," I replied, making sure to include myself in their conversation.

"Well I put some feelers out with my people too just in case," Rose stated.

"You've got people?" I asked sarcastically.

The look Dollar turned around and gave me made me raise my hands in mock surrender. It annoyed the fuck out of me that the bitch had the nerve to chuckle, but I bit my tongue.

"I'll let you know when I hear something. Now that you've made it back in one piece I'm going to bed. This is for you," she said, passing him a glass with dark liquor in it.

I knew that it was juvenile of me to stick my tongue out at her as she walked away, but I did it anyway.

"Your petty is showing sweetheart," he said, chuckling.

"Whatever nigga," I replied, taking the glass from his hand, and quickly swallowing the potent liquid.

I took the glass to the kitchen with me, and tried to figure out what to whip up real fast.

Aryanna

"If you're hungry why don't you just order some food?" he asked, taking a seat at the kitchen counter.

My back was to him so he couldn't see the shit eating grin on my face, but I made sure to erase it before I turned towards him.

"You know how much I love cooking for you. Besides, being able to do it here in Florida brings back some really good memories, and I think that we could really use that right now."

The look in his eyes was a softer one than any I could remember in recent history, and it made my heart flutter wildly.

"So what are you cooking?" he asked.

"What do you have a taste for?"

"That's a loaded question, Tabitha."

"It is, but I bet you that you'll be calling me Honey again before the night's over with."

"Maybe…maybe not. Feed me first, Tabitha."

Chapter 16
Dollar

Years of killing people without mercy, regret, or hesitation made it utterly impossible for me to sleep hard, so the moment I felt her weight on the bed I was awake. My first thought was that Rose had finally come to get the dick, and I was cool with that, but one look at the glowing eyes in the moonlight told me I was wrong. Her movements lacked hesitation, but I could see the uncertainty swimming across her iris as she pulled back the blanket covering me. In my mind I explained away the cold chill I felt as a byproduct of my nakedness being exposed to the air, but her smile said that she knew different. When I didn't say anything she became bolder by quickly dipping her head into my lap, and taking my dick in her mouth like it belonged nowhere else. I'd halfway expected her to be gentle and take her time, but the speed with which her head was bobbing and the power of her suction told me that she had other plans. Within seconds I was harder than gingersnap cookies, and embarrassingly close to finishing before the fun really started.

"Slow down," I whispered, grabbing a fistful of her hair.

She heeded my command, but only barely. Her technique and enthusiasm had my vision swimming in and out of focus with the speed and frequency of an ambulance's emergency lights. On every inch of me that disappeared in between her lips I felt the life she was breathing into me, and it made my heart pound wildly. When I suddenly felt my balls in her mouth I had to fight valiantly to keep my back on the mattress. I found myself letting go of her hair, and using both of my hands to hold onto the sheets like they were the center of gravity. I knew that the twinkle in her eyes was one of silent victory, but I didn't care because all I wanted was fulfillment.

"S-stop playing," I mumbled.

"Never husband."

Her words were spoken softly, but the way she swiftly vaulted on top of me was bold and aggressive, and I liked it. With her hands pressed firmly on my chest she lifted the weight of her entire body like she was levitating, rising just high enough to open her legs and take what she wanted. My dick invaded the tightness of her fortress little by little until we throbbed together in unison, but once that was complete she simply sat there, staring at me mischievously. When I put my hands on her hips, and held her in place while lifting up into her she kept right on smiling. The way that her pussy was squeezing me made it impossible to punish her from this angle, but when I attempted to roll her under me I found out just how strong she was.

"You're-you're playing games," I said, secretly enjoying the torture.

"Am I? Tell me how I'm playing, baby."

Her voice was effortlessly sexy, and the fact that she was swirling her hips to ensure that I hit every wall only made it more so. I didn't say anything because I knew that my voice had lost all ability to sound normal or nonchalant. I knew this was a battle, and I was definitely losing right now, but the way she was riding me nice and slow made it impossible to care.

"C-cat got your tongue big bad Dollar?" she taunted, while moving faster.

"Fuck you."

"You'll get the chance if you s-survive this r-round," she replied.

Whatever I intended to say was forgotten as she switched gears, and broke into a full gallop. In the blink of an eye she became the definition of acting a fool on the ick, and I knew that I was at her mercy. I could taste my climax on my tongue, and I welcomed it like a lovers first kiss, but she must've sensed it because she came to a dead stop.

"Say it, and I'll let you cum."

"Say-say what?" I asked, breathlessly.

"Say m-my name!"

My pride was telling me to resist on principle alone, but I felt like if I didn't cum quickly I might die.

"Honey!" I growled through clenched teeth.

Her smile of victory was brilliant even in the dark, but her momentary distraction cost her. With a ninja's speed I rolled to my left with her, and I didn't stop until we hit the floor hard. I could tell by the stunned expression on her face that she was surprised, and I knew that the tide had turned. I quickly slammed her on her back, moved on top of her, and rammed my dick back inside her. In less than ten strokes she came all over my dick with my name rolling off her tongue like prayers of sacrifice. From that point forward the concept of time had no meaning, nor was important, as we fucked each other every way possible until the sun chased away all of the darkness. I lost track of how many times I came and where I came, but after the last joint climax I fell into the deepest sleep I'd ever known. When I awoke I was in bed alone, even though I could still smell Honey all over my sheets and skin. The solitude demanded that I analyze what had happened and what it all meant, which was what I really didn't wanna do. Nevertheless I still found myself asking the million dollar question of what happens next. Despite the fire and passion in the bedroom we still had major issues, and good sex didn't make those go away. I didn't know that anything could fix our problems, but the first question that I needed to ask myself was did I want things fixed? The ugly truth was that we'd both done some ugly shit to each other. I'd never been in the business of forgiving anyone, but if there was one person that my usual tactics didn't apply to it was her. God help me, but the crazy bitch still had a hold on me! Admitting this made me smile ruefully as I got out of the bed, and went to the bathroom to shower. Thirty minutes later the scent of the animalistic fuck fest between me and Honey was gone, despite the memory being fresh in my mind. As soon as I opened the bedroom door I smelled the sweetness of cinnamon rolls pulling me towards the kitchen, and I didn't fight it.

"Bout time you got up nigga," Rose said, using her fingers to rip apart a cinnamon roll.

My eyes went past her smiling face and landed squarely on the smirk Honey was sporting. It was obvious that she was satisfied with her accomplishment of making me say her name, but we both knew that her voice was a little scratchy from screaming too.

"Those cinnamon rolls smell good," I said, moving towards the full plate on the counter.

"You'll never taste anything sweeter," Honey replied.

The laughter that bubbled up in my throat was involuntary, and I couldn't stop it from coming out.

"Don't choke," Rose said, laughing.

The sound of Aubrey's ringtone going off from the phone in my pocket froze the laughter in my throat. I pulled it out quickly and answered without saying a word.

"You're plan worked. She's been spotted in Daytona beach Florida with Katie...but there's a slight problem," Aubrey said hurriedly.

"What's the problem?"

Hearing me ask this question made Rose and Honey look squarely at me with the battle readiness of a seasoned solider.

"The police only stopped her and questioned her, but they didn't detain her or take Kyla because Katie produced Kyla's birth certificate with Katie listed as the mom. The spot for father is marked unknown, so as far as the authorities are concerned the Amber Alert was a hoax since Kyla is with her only parent," Aubrey replied.

I hadn't considered this possibility when I'd told her to issue the Amber Alert, but all still wasn't lost.

"How long ago did they let Katie go?" I asked.

"About ten minutes ago, and of course you know that I've been tracking her movements. The car she's in is headed in the direction of Fort Lauderdale, but I just got confirmation that Anthony's widow, Clarrissa, ordered her private jet to be fueled and ready."

I could feel the blood in my veins going colder than any reptile as the knowledge that this info brought set in. I knew first hand that having money and power made running a more attractive option than facing your greatest fear, but I wasn't about to let that bitch get away that easy.

"Where's the plane?" I asked.

"A private airfield about an hour from you. I'm shooting the directions to the GPS in your car."

"Uh, send it to my phone because it's not safe to drive the Wrath anymore," I said, giving Honey a knowing look.

"I'm sure I don't even wanna know, but I'll send them to your phone now. Is there anything else you need?"

"Yeah, make sure that no matter what she don't get away with my daughter," I said, hanging up.

"What's the plan?" Honey asked immediately.

"She's headed for a private jet, and if she makes it then the sky is the limit."

"Go get her," Rose said, tossing me a set of car keys.

In an instant the Honey that was about her housewife cooking shit was put away, and I could see the monster in her eyes surface.

"Let's go," I said, leading the way back to my bedroom.

We quickly packed what we needed in a leather duffle bag, and within ten minutes I was behind the wheel of Rose's cherry red 2020 Porsche 911 GT, with the pedal to the floor.

"Input the location into the car's GPS," I said, tossing Honey my phone, while shifting gears rapidly.

The horsepower and speed under my fingertips reminded me of my Ferrari, which made me think about Iree. I'd harnessed and suppressed all the emotion I'd felt about losing her, but little by little, mile by mile, I opened the tomb inside me and let the hurt seep out. I had no idea what I was gonna do to Katie when I caught her, I just knew that she wouldn't live beyond this day if I had anything to say about it.

"At this speed we'll be there in thirty-five minutes," Honey said.

"Ok, call Aubrey and find out where Katie and Kyla are. I want to intercept them before they get to the airfield."

While she was doing that I was thinking about how I would console Kyla once her mom was dead and gone. I knew how much Kyla loved her mother, but not even that was enough to save her ass this time. When I heard Honey say something about straight ahead, I focused in on her conversation.

"Is it just one escort?" Honey asked.

Whatever response she got made her nod her head, hang up, and reach inside the duffle bag at her feet.

"What's up?" I asked.

"They should be not far ahead of us on the opposite side of the road because the airfield is on our left, which is their right. Somewhere along the way she picked up a police escort though, two cars total, one in front, and the other in the back."

"Money can buy you anything, especially cops, so I'm not surprised. Nor do I care," I said seriously.

"I figured you'd say that."

The meaning behind her response was clear by the speed with which she was loading the AR-15 automatic pistol in her hands. Once she had the eleven shot clip loaded with hollow tips she placed it in my lap and moved on to the AK-74 in her lap. I saw the flashing lights long before I spotted the police cruiser less than a mile away from us, but the sight of them was enough to make me put the pedal to the floor. When the lights suddenly vanished I felt the ache in my jaw as I clinched my teeth in anger, while willing the car to either go faster or develop wings. When I got to the turn I had the Porsche up on two wheels sliding thru the intersection, and the speedometer was stuck on 150 mph. the tires screamed murderously as they fought for traction. All four wheels hit the ground, and suddenly we were inside a rocket because we took off. It seemed like in a matter of seconds the flashing lights were once again in my sights, and before I knew it I had us close enough to read the license plates on the cop car.

"How do you wanna handle it?" she asked, looking over at me.

"There's only one way to handle it."

With that said I rolled down my window, and stuck the AR-15 out of it. I took a deep breath while sighting my target, and then I let my gun breathe for me.

Chapter 17
Honey

Seeing the cops slump down in their seats right before their car swerved off the road, and smacked head first into a tree made me laugh. Not wanting to let Dollar have all the fun had me pushing the button to send my own window down, and sticking the Draco out into the daylight.

"Don't shoot at the town car, Kyla is in there," he said quickly.

"I know that Dameian, now get me up alongside the other cop car."

He should've had to pass the car carrying Katie and Kyla, but apparently taking out the first cop car had got the others attention because they were now falling back to protect the civilians. As soon as I got a clear shot I started pumping bullets at the ones who swore to serve and protect. It was actually funny how easily my bullets ripped through the cops car, and within minutes they joined their fallen comrades.

"Two down, one to go," Dollar said, continuing to chase the last car in front of us.

I reloaded the clip on my gun, preparing for whatever happened next.

"When they stop I want you to grab Kyla, and put her in this car," he said.

"I got her, don't worry."

The sight of the locked gate looming in front of us had me preparing to jump out and rush the car, but whoever was driving decided not to stop.

"I think she knows it's you back here," I said, chuckling.

"You think?"

Even as he asked the question he power shifted, and catapulted us through the hole in the fence behind them. I could hear the jets engines already spinning idlily, which meant that our window of opportunity was small.

"We've got company," I said, pointing at the security patrol headed towards us.

"Deal with it!"

I wasted no time leaning half of my body out of the window, and sending hot slugs to greet the blue and white Ford Explorer. It took two three round bursts to lift the hood off of its hinges, and send it flying backwards through the windshield. The driver lost control instantly and trying to overcorrect resolved in the SUV rolling like a pair of shook dice. The town car barely avoided colliding with the SUV, but it did manage to put some more space in between us.

"I'm going for the trees!" I yelled.

I didn't wait for a response before I let off four shots that shredded the right rear tire. The car suddenly fishtailed wildly, but the driver recovered and prevented an accident. A few seconds later they slid to a stop at the bottom of the stairway of the waiting G3. Before anyone could open a door we'd slid to a stop behind them, and hopped out with our guns ready.

"Give me Kyla, Katie," Dollar yelled.

I don't really think that he expected a response, and he wasn't disappointed. The sound of approaching sirens meant time was of the essence though, which meant that talking was powerless.

"Cover me," I said, advancing on the car with my gun up.

I'd almost made it to the rear bumper when the front passenger door opened, and my beloved sister got out. I would've dropped her where she stood, had it not been for my niece clinging to her.

"You're really gonna hide behind your daughter, you weak ass bitch?" I asked with disgust.

"If this is the only way to get her dad to listen, then so be it. Dollar I-I didn't mean for anything to happen to Iree, I swear—"

"Shut up you lying bitch!" he screamed.

I could tell by the way that he was shaking that he was barely maintaining his composure, and I knew where that would lead him. Out of my peripheral vision I spotted my father's widow step out of the car, but if she thought she was getting away then she was mistaken. I tapped the trigger twice and turned her face into ruined hamburger.

"Give me Kyla, Katie, it's over and you know it," I said.

"Dollar please just listen to me! I'm begging you on the love that we have for our daughter to hear me out, and believe me. I didn't wanna kill Iree."

"You didn't?" he asked in a calmer tone.

"No baby, I didn't mean to kill her. Why would I do that when I know how much you love her? I love you Dollar, and no lie that Tabitha tells you will change that. Please don't let her tear us apart with her bullshit because she's the same bitch who shot us and left us for dead."

Hearing her words made me tighten my grip on the gun in my hand, but I didn't utter a word.

"Oh I know exactly who Honey is and what she did, so trust me when I tell you that you'll die by my hand because it's what I want. Now give me my fucking daughter."

I could hear the growl in his voice, and it was a warning to anyone with common sense. Dollar was definitely on the edge!

"I-I can't give her to you Dollar. If I do that then you'll kill me," Katie said.

It was on the tip of my tongue to tell her that she was absolutely fucking right, but before I knew it she was moving. With Kyla still clutched firmly in her grip she made a mad dash up the stairs of the jet, and disappeared inside. I wanted to blow her back off so bad that I could taste it, but I knew that shooting her could also hurt Kyla. When I looked over at Dollar I could tell that he was thinking the same thing, so we did the only thing left for us to do. We followed her.

"Get us in the air," he said, looking at me and nodding towards the cockpit.

I really wanted to follow him to the back of the plane and participate in killing that bitch, but the sounds of the sirens were getting louder.

"Take off!" I demanded, bursting into the cockpit with my gun out in front of me.

The terror on the pilot's face was easy to read, but luckily for him it didn't hinder his work performance. Within moments I felt the plane shift beneath my feet, and the taxing was underway.

"If you stop this plane for any reason, or if you radio for help, I can promise you a very painful death for you and everyone that you love in this world," I stated emotionlessly.

I didn't wait for a response before spinning on my heels, and heading in the direction that I had last seen Dollar going. When I made it to the seats I pulled up short, baffled by what I was seeing. Katie was sitting in the far right side corner of the plane with Kyla in her lap, and Dollar was sitting right next to them playing with Kyla. The scene was so disproportionate to the gun waving stare down that had just taken place on the tarmac that I was almost believing that I had imagined the whole damn thing.

"Uh…what the fuck Dollar?" I asked, genuinely confused.

"I'm just trying to keep my daughter calm Honey, but don't worry because Katie is still gonna get everything that she deserves."

I could still hear the determination and pain in his voice, coating every word spoken, but the look on Katie's face made me uneasy. She had the nerve to be smirking, like she didn't believe that her ending was just around the next bend in the road. It absolutely was though because even if she somehow managed to change Dollar's mind, she didn't have a chance in hell of changing mine. I slowly took the seat across from them, and stared at the spectacle that this rescue mission had turned into. I couldn't tell if my heart was hammering in my chest due to adrenaline or just plain disgust, not either would allow me to loosen the grip that I had on my pistol. When it became physically nauseating to watch Dollar entertain Kyla I looked out the window, and counted the number of security cars rushing towards us. The plane quickly picked up speed, and within moments we were airborne on our way to nowhere fast.

"What's the plan bae?" I asked, once the plane levelled off from its steep climb.

"Bae?" Katie echoed, looking over at Dollar before she looked at me with hate in her eyes.

"Yes bitch, Bae! As in that's my nigga right there, and you will never have him again. Any question?" I asked, I could tell that she had a lot that she wanted to say, but the pistol in my hand made her think twice.

"The plan is simple, I'm taking my daughter and giving her the best life that I can. Anyone who stands in the way of that will die."

Dollar spoke in a tone of calm assuredness, and the silent tears rolling down Katie's face told me that she understood that there was absolutely nothing that she could say or do to change his mind. I knew that it was petty of me to smile, but I did it anyway.

"Do-do I get one last request?" she asked, looking over at Dollar with eyes begging for mercy that she didn't deserve.

"A request? You can't be serious! After what you did," he replied.

"I fucked up Dollar, and I know that, but I'm still your daughter's mother just like little miss innocent sitting over there all high and mighty. It's obvious that you granted her some type of reprieve, and what she did was worse than what I did. So the least that you can do is give me one last request."

Her lame plea made me chuckle, but the laughter quickly died in my throat when I saw that this nigga was actually contemplating what she was saying.

"Dameian I know that you're not even thinking about giving this lying, murdering, nothing ass bitch anything except for several well placed hot bullets," I said, with mounting frustration.

"Shut up and let me think Honey, damn!"

I had to bite a hole in my tongue so that I didn't utter the foul shit that was on my mind. I loved Dollar in a way that I never had any other man, but right now I detested the weak nigga sitting across from me. The man that he was now was definitely not the one that I'd married. The man I'd married had an iron will, and didn't second guess one single decision when it came to killing someone, but this nigga...this nigga seemed so different by comparison.

"What is it that you want Katie, and if you say some dumb shit I promise you that I'm gonna make your going away party extra painful," he vowed.

"I know that I have to answer for what I did...nothing in life goes unpunished. With that being said I think it's only fair that Tabitha be the one to serve me my death sentence...or get served."

"What the fuck do you mean or get served bitch?" I asked quickly.

"Just what it sounds like sis. Winner takes all. If you kill me then I'm gone and you can claim your place on the throne next to the king that we both love...but if I kill you then I get it all. I get to live happily ever after with Dollar and our kids because that's what I deserve. You're not scared of me, right?"

"There's never been a day in life when I was ever scared of you bitch, and today ain't about to be the first. What you're not gonna do is try to weasel your way out of what you have coming to you, so if you wanna die by my hand I'm all too happy to grant you that last wish," I replied genuinely.

There were no more words necessary, which left us both looking at Dollar expectantly. His dark eyes were locked on mine, and I could feel the anger and hatred that he kept bottled up inside as if it were his fingers touching me gently on the cheek. The look he was giving me said one thing, and that was that if I chose to accept this challenge then it was a fight to the death.

"I got this Dollar," I said, reassuringly.

He still didn't say a word, but after a few more moments he nodded slightly to let us know that he was with it. Without a word I got up out of my seat, and headed back towards the cockpit to have a word with the pilot.

"I-I didn't radio for help, I swear!" he said shakily.

"That's good, and if you do what I tell you next then you might just make it home before dinner. I want you to take us to Mexico, and make sure that you stay below any radar detection."

"Yes-yes ma'am," he replied.

Closing the door, I turned around and made my way back to my seat with a smile on my face.

"Do you wanna let me in on whatever it is that you're planning?" Dollar asked.

"I mean it's nothing serious, I just told the pilot where to go so that we can get this shit over with.

"Let me guess, you wanna go back to Mississippi so that you can finish this shit where you failed to do it last time?" Katie asked sarcastically.

"Nah, not quite. I was thinking that me and my family could take a quick vacation after I dispose of you, so why not already be in Mexico," I said, smiling.

"You dispose of me??? That's funny as fuck bitch, almost as funny as the last bitch who thought she could fuck with me."

Before I could say or do anything to respond to what Katie had said Dollar hit her with a short jab that stunned her enough for her to relax her grip on Kyla. With the speed of a seasoned hunter Dollar grabbed Kyla, tossed her into my lap, and had his hand wrapped around Katie's throat before she could move an inch. I didn't have to be told how this was gonna go, or that Kyla didn't need to see this, so I got up swiftly and headed for the bedroom at the rear of the plane.

"Mommyyyy!" Kyla hollered, reaching back towards Katie.

"It's ok sweetie, your daddy just needs to have a private talk with your mom. She's ok though, so shhhhh."

"M-mommy!" she whined, trying to scramble out of my arms.

I held on tight to her and kept walking until we made it inside the room. Once I had us inside with the door closed I sat on the bed with her in my lap, pulled out my phone, and found some videos on YouTube for her to watch. At first she didn't want to look or even entertain anything besides being back with her mom, but I kept forcing the phone on her and eventually the funny videos got her attention. The sigh of relief that escaped from my throat was genuine, but I had no illusions that making her forget Katie in the long run was gonna be any kind of easy. I stayed in the room with Kyla, enjoying and preserving her innocence until sleep finally came through and assisted me with her. Only when I was sure that she wouldn't wake up from my movement did I dare to gently lay her on the bed, and creep out of the room. I was careful to open and close the door extra softly, but the moment that I was on the other side of it my brain shifted gears while registering the smell of blood in the air. I didn't hear any voices, not even whispers, and that made the hair on the back of my neck stand up straight. When I made it back to where I'd left Dollar and Katie I paused next to my seat, and took in the scene in front of me. Katie was on the floor, naked, curled into a ball, and bleeding freely from several different wounds. Her breathing was so shallow that I had to pay close attention to the subtle rise and fall of her body in order to determine that she was still alive.

"Almost stole the show, didn't you?" I asked, looking at Dollar.

He didn't respond, but instead lit the cigarette in between his lips and leaned back in the chair. The sound of Katie crying was faint, but still recognizable for what it was over the jet's engines.

"Don't cry now bitch, the time for that is coming soon enough," I said, smiling.

I could tell that it was painful for her to move, but she still managed to uncurl enough to look up at me. I thought she was gonna say some slick shit, but instead she cleared her throat and spit a glob of bloody saliva on my leg.

"You ain't woman enough to kill me bitch!" I laughed at her display of bravado.

Then I raised my foot and brought it down on her face.

Chapter 18
Dollar
Five hours later

I'd never known so many mixed emotions as I could feel coursing through my veins in this moment. The pain from losing Iree was definitely real and present, which only increased my thrust for revenge, but the sound of Kyla crying for her mother was still ringing in my ears. It had taken everything in me not to kill Katie when we were on the plane, and the only reason that I hadn't done it was because Kyla was too close to the situation. Right now I had all of us hidden behind the wall of a mini mansion in Tijuana, Mexico, and Kyla was enjoying playing with the kids of the maids who took care of the house, but I still felt like she was too close. I didn't want her to have any memory of her mother dying, especially not that of her last day on earth. So I did what I had to do to distract my daughter while Honey and Katie prepared for their show-down. At first Katie's request had taken me by surprise, but the more that I thought about it the more I thought it was fitting. I couldn't deny that despite all that had happened I still had feelings for both women. That didn't necessarily mean that I would ultimately end up with either of them, but this high noon style show down would be entertaining if nothing else. Deep down I think that Katie just wanted to kill Honey before she died, because surely she knew that I couldn't let her live no matter what. I just couldn't do that because if I did then that would mean that Iree had died for absolutely nothing, and that's all her life would be worth. Nothing. So for me the real question was what happened once all of this shit was over with? The feeling of my phone vibrating in my pocket interrupted my contemplation of that question.

"What's good, sis?" I asked, pulling the phone out of my pocket, and answering it.

"I'm just checking in and making sure that you're ok, or as ok as you can be given the circumstances."

"I'm aight, I guess, just ready for this shit to be over for good. I'm tired Aubrey."

"You know, I've heard you say that before, but it feels different this time around. I don't think it's just the physical aspect of you that's worn down, I think this has cost you more mentally than you could've expected."

It was on the tip of my tongue to tell her that I didn't need or appreciate her psychoanalyzing me, but I let it go because there was too much truth in her statement to fight it. I'd never be over the fact that Iree was gone, or that Katie had taken her from me. The fact that Katie would die shortly didn't even offer the usual amount of joy one would associate with revenge, so I knew that I would never put this behind me. I was self-aware enough to admit that I was broken beyond repair, which left me asking myself what was next for me. For a fleeting second I saw me eating a bullet, but I quickly pushed that thought from my mind.

"What it costs is of no consequence because all debts will be paid in full shortly. Trust me. I appreciate you being worried about me, but you know that I keep on pushing no matter what happens because life is ten percent what happens to you and ninety percent how you react to it," I said emotionlessly.

"True enough, but you're still human. Don't lose that."

"I lost that a long time ago, but I know you didn't call me to wax poetic, so what's really good?" I asked, hoping to change the topic.

"Well let's start with your getaway. You've got half the world looking for you, but so far there's been no solid information given about you or Honey's whereabouts. I think that it's safe to say that you got away clean, and now that you're no longer on the shores of North America I suggest you never return for any reason. With that thought in mind, I need to know where you want me to meet you with the kids, and what do you want me to tell Rain about all of this stuff?"

In the chaos I had forgotten that Rain had no idea that Iree was dead, and now here I was about to possibly let her mom get taken from her too.

"I don't know, and I honestly can't think about that right now sis so just duck her until I figure out the next move."

"I tried that, but she's been blowing my phones up because she hasn't heard from Iree or her mom. You know like I do that she can be just as impulsive as her mother, and that's the last thing that we need right now," Aubrey replied.

I knew the truth when I heard it, but even if I didn't I still knew firsthand how quickly Rain would go rouge without considering the danger she was putting herself in. Now wasn't the time for that shit.

"I can handle Rain, and I'll call you with a meet up location sometime tonight. How are the kids doing anyway?" I asked.

"They're good. You know that I still have all of Honey's kids under constant surveillance, and little Dorian is the sweetest baby I've ever known in my life. It's hard to believe that he's you and Honey's son considering how crazy you two are."

"I won't even take that as an insult because you're taking care of my little man, but you better watch yourself."

The sound of her laughter floated over the phone line, and I could picture her face in this moment in my mind. That made me miss her more than a little bit, but I pushed all of that aside as Honey entered the bedroom where I was laying across the king sized bed.

"I'll call you soon sis. Kiss my son for me."

"I got you bruh. Be safe please, and I'll see you soon."

My eyes locked with Honey's as I hung up the phone and sat up on the bed.

"How's Dorian?" she asked.

"He's fine, and so are all the rest of the kids. Rain is on Aubrey's ass right now because she ain't heard from you or Iree."

"Do you want me to call her?" she asked.

"I think that you might have to in order to keep her from doing some crazy shit…plus it's probably a good idea considering what's about to take place."

Ever since Katie had challenged her, Honey had been moving with a nonchalance, but I could tell by the look in her eyes that she was considering what it meant if this shit didn't come out in her favor. It wasn't exactly fear that I saw swimming in her iris, but it wasn't that cocky self-confidence that I'd come to know as part of her fighter's spirit.

"Dollar I need to ask a favor of you, and I know that I have no right to do that, but I'm gonna ask anyway."

"You don't gotta ask that, I got all of your kids no matter what. You should already know that."

She nodded her head while adverting her eyes so that I wouldn't see the tears that were suddenly clouding her vision. I couldn't explain the feelings in me at this moment that had my chest tight, but I felt for Honey, and I still mourned the love that would never be for us. When she finally looked back at me I could see that she knew the ghetto fairy tale that we envisioned for us was coming to an end. The sight of her heart breaking in her eyes was something that I knew I would never forget for as long as I lived.

"Come here," I said, standing up.

There was no hesitation as she walked into my arms, and held me as tight as she had the very first time that we had made love to one another. The sweet smell of her skin tickled my nose as memory after memory flooded my brain in waves, making it harder to breathe with each one. I could feel my arms tightening around her as the seconds dragged on, and I felt my heart beating harder in sync with hers.

"We could've been great," she whispered into my chest.

"I know bae, I know,"

When I looked down into her upturned face I felt a piece of me disappear with every tear that slid down her face, and before I could stop myself I was kissing those tears away. Her mouth sought mine, and I gave her my lips to do with as she pleased. The hunger in her kisses was startling at first, but it quickly brought mine to the surface, and then nothing existed except for us. The negotiation between our tongues was so fierce and thorough that I had no idea when we undressed each other, but suddenly I felt the heat of her flesh on mine. With ease I lifted her into my arms and held her close, not releasing the hold that my mouth had on hers, while spinning her around so that I could lay her on the bed. The moment that her back hit the comforter was synonymous with my dick pushing inside her warm pussy. I only gave her a few seconds to adjust to my invasion before I pulled back out, and dove deeper with the purpose of making her remember me forever. The way her pussy juices drenched my dick instantly had my eyes rolling up into my skull in search of the barcode on my brain, and I loved it.

"Dameian," she moaned passionately, while locking her legs around my waist.

I wanted to howl with pleasure because of how she was clamping her pussy walls down on my dick rhythmically, but I bit her neck instead while fucking her faster. Every stroke rattled the headboard off the wall, creating an unmistakable sound that echoed, but I couldn't slow down, let up, or pause in stride. I was a man on a mission. It only took a few pounding blows before the trembling started in her toes, and the opening bell of orgasm was rung in the fight.

"Fuck!" she squeaked, scratching my back hard enough to make a wolverine proud.

I knew that the first climax would open her completely to me, so I fed her harder strokes that only left the whites of her eyes visible. Every aftershock that rocked her body rolled through me like an electrical current, making it harder and harder to hold off my own climax. The sensations shooting through me reminded me of the pleasurable pain that came with edging, and that brought out the savage side of my dick game.

"D-d-d—"

My hand clamping down on her neck kept my name stuck in her throat, but I could read the clear bliss in her eyes as they changed colors. Every time I dove deep I made sure to squeeze her neck tighter, making it hard to breathe, while increasing the pleasure she felt. When her eyes got as big around as a softball I thought that the epic climax was within her grasp, but the heavy blow to the back of my head brought me back to reality.

"Step out of the pussy my nigga," Katie said, pushing me off of Honey.

I couldn't understand why I was suddenly seeing double, but once I comprehended that Katie was holding a brick in her hand I understood better. My hand went to my head as I struggled to stand up, and the sight of bright red blood coating my fingertips took me from horny to hostile instantly.

"Bitch are you cr-crazy?" I asked, in disbelief.

"You already know the answer to that question Dollar."

I lunged at Katie with the intention of beating her entire ass, but she easily sidestepped my advance, and smacked me with the brick again. This time my vision swam like someone was playing with the light switch, but luckily my power didn't completely go out. In that moment I made the decision that Honey was just gonna have to forgive me because if I could make it to my gun this bitch was all types of dead. I turned to my left to search for the pants I'd had on, and I spotted them at the foot of the bed. I never got to take a step towards them though because before I knew it, I felt another blow to the back of the head, and I was falling. I put my arms out in front of me to brace myself, but the ground was coming to fast.

I thought it would hurt when I hit the ground face first, but I never felt it. I didn't feel anything.

Chapter 19
Honey

The afterglow of my orgasm had me moving at snail speed, but I still managed to scramble out of bed and advance on Katie before she could turn the brink on me.

"I hate a cockblocker," I said, throwing a right hook.

My punch connected flush with her chin, and I heard the bones in her jaw grinding in loud protest. I'd been in enough fights to know what it meant when someone's eyes lit up the way that hers were at this moment, and so I went for the knock out with a follow up left jab. When my fist connected with nothing except air I was confused, but that quickly wore off when I felt her land a short jab of her own to my nose.

"I told you before that I was faster than you bitch," she said, taking a step back and squaring up.

"And I proved then that it was a lie, so give me your best shot, pussy."

When she smiled at me I knew that she actually thought that I was prepared to play defense, and that's what I wanted her to think. I switched to a southpaw stance, and fired two right jabs with lightning speed that blew her two front teeth out of her mouth like pieces of fallen candy.

"Now you look the part, you hillbilly bitch," I said smiling.

The rage in her eyes was instantaneous, and preceded her reckless barrage of punches in a way that allowed me to counter her movements without really trying. I ducked under her four punch combination, and fired a left-right duo of my own that knocked her into a wall hard enough to relieve her of the air in her lungs. The look of shock on her face was comical, but I didn't let up in my attack. I advanced intending to kick her squarely in the chest, only to have her grab my foot in mid-air and flip me on my face.

"You should learn to keep your legs closed bitch," she growled.

I opened my mouth to respond, but all I could do was scream as I felt her twist my ankle mercilessly until the bone snapped like an animal cracker. I couldn't stop the tears that sprang to my eyes any more than I could the pain I was feeling, but neither thing made me helpless. I used all my strength to kick her right in her pussy, and I was rewarded with the sweet howl of pain that passed her lips and hung in the air. I knew that the pain wasn't nearly as severe for a woman as it was for a man, which meant my window of opportunity was smaller. I didn't waste a minute though. I dove blindly over the bed for my pile of clothes in search of the pistol that I knew was there. No sooner than I felt the comforting grip of the gun in my palm I felt my head being pulled in the opposite direction.

"You pulling hair now bitch," I growled, trying to elbow her, while bringing the gun around to point it at her face.

"Whatever it takes."

I almost had her in my sights, but when she stomped on my already shattered ankle I saw dark spots swim into my vision, causing me to fight for consciousness. There was no doubt in my mind that if I faded to black I was way past dead, so I fought with everything I had left in me to remain conscious. The game of tug of war was intense and serious, if the expression on her face was and indicator. The smile of death went from her lips all the way up to her eyes, and I knew that it was kill or be killed. Thinking quickly, I squeezed off two shots from my gun, knowing that the deafening sound of it firing would work to my advantage. As soon as she winced distractedly I kneed her in the stomach, and threw a right uppercut that landed right on her chin. In comical movie fashion she came off of her feet, going airborne, and landed flat on her back next to Dollar. I took careful aim at her left knee and, then blew a neat hole in it. The smile on my face only widened as she screamed out in pain while clutching her leg, and rolling around on the floor.

"That probably burns a little, huh?" I asked, sarcastically.

Before she could answer I sighted down the barrel at her right knee, and removed it from her body just as ruthlessly. I loved how her screams got louder and took a hysterical edge. I saw Dollar's eyes flutter open, and since I knew that Katie couldn't go anywhere or do anything I hobbled over to help him.

"You ok bae?" I asked, leaning down to help him up.

"Wh-what the fuck happened?"

"Well, you were giving me some of that good dick, when this nothing ass bitch decided to rudely interrupt us by hitting you over the head with a brick."

At first his eyes had the shine of disbelief in them, but as he quickly evaluated the situation I saw him put the pieces of the puzzle together. He took the gun from my hand, and turned it on her, but before he could pull the trigger the bedroom door opened.

"Everything good senor?"

The question came from a short, stocky Mexican who was holding a AR-15 pistol like it was his newborn son.

"Yeah, we're good Jose. Just handling some family business before we leave. Is my daughter ok?" Dollar asked.

"Si, she is in the kitchen eating right now. Would you like me to bring her to you?"

This seemed like a dumb question to me, but I understood that the cartel believed in desensitizing their kids to murder very early in their lives. We didn't move like that though.

"No Jose, let her eat. We'll be down in a minute," I replied.

He nodded once, and backed out of the room as smoothly as he'd came. Katie's screams had turned to a pathetic crying that only made me realize how much her and I really weren't alike. Siblings we may have been, but I was cut from a different cloth than she was.

"Shoot that bitch, and let's get on with our lives husband."

Dollar looked at me and smiled before turning his attention back to Katie…but he didn't pull the trigger.

"What's the holdup bae?" I asked, confused.

"Nothing…it's nothing, I was just thinking."

"What's there to think about? I mean, she killed your daughter, and tried to kidnap your other daughter. You and I both know that that's grounds to die in the worst way possible, so she's getting off easy for real since you're only putting a bullet in her brain," I said, looking at her in disgust.

"You're absolutely right…"

"If I'm right then why the fuck are you hesitating?" I asked, with mounting frustration.

True enough, he was still pointing the gun at her face, but the fact that he hadn't pulled the trigger at least once was starting to give me a bad feeling. There was no question of whether or not she had to die, so I didn't understand what the goddamn waiting game was about.

"Dollar?"

"He-he can't do it," Katie said softly.

"Oh no, I can absolutely do it, and you know that I can because I've done it before."

"Then what's the problem?" I asked.

"Kyla."

The way that Dollar's shoulders slumped when Katie said their daughter's name told me that there was nothing but truth in that statement. The most ruthless assassin in the northern hemisphere was about to be brought to his knees by a toddler.

"Kyla will be fine Dollar, and you know that. You and I will be the best parents that she could ever hope for, and she will forget all about having this worthless bitch for a mother."

"Will she though?" Katie asked, looking directly at Dollar.

"Yes she'll forget you bitch, just like she did when you went to prison. She barely even knows you, and we all know that I'm a much better mother than you could ever be," I replied angrily.

"What do you think Dollar? Will our daughter forget me?" Katie asked.

"I-I don't know."

The uncertainty in his voice made my skin crawl, and sent off all sorts of warning bells in my mind, but I kept it cool.

"You can entertain this bullshit if you want to, but I'm not. You know that all of us are better off with this bitch dead, so stop playing and pull the fucking trigger!" I demanded impatiently.

He still didn't move, and that told me all that I needed to know. I calmly moved to his pile of clothes, and riffled through them until I found what I was looking for.

"I see that I have to wear pants in this relationship now," I said, raising my gun and aiming it at Katie.

The terror returned to her eyes instantly, and I liked that because I knew that I would remember that look forever.

"Hell is waiting on you bitch," I said sweetly.

The sound of the pistol going off once again echoed around the room, and then the screaming resumed. The only problem was that I was the one screaming.

Chapter 20
Dollar

The smoking pistol in my hand seemed unreal, but the way Honey was hollering and holding her arm told me that I had definitely shot her. It hadn't been a conscious thought to turn the gun on her, but I knew that until I figured out what to do with Katie I had to stop Honey from doing something she couldn't undo. Did Katie deserve to die? Absolutely! My mind was circling around how her death would affect our child though. I could still hear Kyla's cries for her mom when shit had gotten out of hand on the plane, and in my heart I knew that she wouldn't easily forget the woman who birthed her. It was true that Honey could and would treat her just like any of our other kids, but it wouldn't be the same. With Katie dead nothing would be the same, and that was a reality I was coming to grips with in this moment.

"You-you bastard! You fucking shot me!" Honey yelled.

"Yes, I did shoot you, but only to get your attention so that you wouldn't shoot her."

"She deserves to be shot!" Honey cried.

"I can't argue that point, and I won't. I just know that my daughter deserves all the happiness and love that I never got, and so does my son for that matter. We've lived our lives, so when do we start to think about the children that depend on us for their survival?" I asked.

If I hadn't been the one talking I wouldn't have believed the words coming out of my mouth, but even as I said them I knew how right they were. Everything in me wanted to avenge Iree's death, but in all honesty the best way for me to do that was to give her siblings a better life than I had her. She should've never died the way that she did, and she also shouldn't have lived the way that she did either. The guilt for both was mine, and this was the way to atone for all of it. The question was how did I make these two strong willed women see my point.

"Honey I know that you loved Iree as much as I did, and you want Katie to pay for that, but is killing her really payment? Is changing the course of Kyla's life how you want to make shit right for Iree? And Katie, do you really want my son to grow up without all the love that we can give him just like our daughter did? Do you want him to be another angry, bitter black man like his father, and his grandfather?"

My questions were met with silence, but I could see the contemplation through the pain in both women's eyes. None of us was perfect or without blood on our hands, but we were all capable of change if we wanted it bad enough.

"So what are you say-saying?" Honey asked, wincing in obvious pain.

"I'm saying that we can make this work, and be one big dysfunctional family of sorts," I replied.

"I n-need a doctor," Katie mumbled from her spot on the floor.

When I looked down at her I noticed all the blood that she'd lost, and I knew that this conversation would have to wait until later.

"Honey get dressed as best you can while I get our friends to call a doctor," I said, hurriedly pulling on my boxers and shorts.

I made sure to take both guns with me so that an unfortunate accident couldn't happen while I was gone.

When I came out of the room I found Jose standing at the end of the hallway next to a middle aged white man, who looked very out of place in this environment.

"You need a doctor senor?" Jose asked before I could utter a word.

"Si, very quickly," I replied.

The white man wasted no time moving in my direction, and on past me into the room. I took a moment to get my thoughts together because lord only knew when I would get the chance again. The doctor stayed in the room with them for about ten minutes before poking his head back out, and speaking rapid Spanish to Jose. I wasn't green by any means, so I knew that he'd told Jose to bring the car around so that we could move them to a different location. I trusted the hospitals in Mexico about as much as I trusted the water, but I had a feeling that wherever we were going was some place private, and clean. Jose disappeared and then reappeared a few minutes later to help me carry both of my baby mama's down to the waiting Chevy Suburban. Once everyone was loaded up we moved out at a high rate of speed. Fifteen minutes later we arrived at a condo in the middle of the city that had been converted into a makeshift emergency room. The place was clean, but the work of sewing up their wounds was slow and tedious. Despite Honey and Katie being in good hands I still insisted on staying with them every step of the way for moral support. We didn't talk, but the silence wasn't awkward either. I could tell that everyone was locked into their own thoughts, and that was okay as long as we weren't trying to kill each other. Two hours later we were back in the safety of the mansion, and we were all in the same bedroom where shit had gone crazy a short time ago.

"You think that you can have both of us, don't you?" Honey asked, laying down on the bed and looking at the ceiling.

"I think that we can all co-exist for the betterment of our kids," I replied neutrally.

"There's no music on Dameian, so stop dancing," Katie said, laying down beside Honey.

"I'm not dancing, I'm just answering the question that should've been asked."

"Oh, so you don't think that it's a valid question to ask if you think that you can keep fucking us both?" Honey asked.

"It's definitely a valid question," Katie chimed in.

I shook my head while trying to hide the smile on my face, as I thought of a way around this entire conversation.

"I never said nor thought that I could have both of you," I replied.

"So then you've either already made a decision in your mind, or you're ready to make one. That's interesting," Katie said.

"It is interesting. So who's it gonna be Dameian?" Honey asked.

"If I have to choose then I choose…neither."

"Neither?" they said in unison.

"That's right, neither. We can all just be parents to our kids, put them first, and live our best lives with whoever we find that can fit into this crazy world of ours," I replied genuinely.

The silence that followed my statement was thick, and the looks on their faces told me that they thought what I said was complete and utter bullshit.

"I can tell that you two weren't expecting that response, huh?"

"No, because it's a bullshit response and you know it," Honey stated.

"Bullshit in what way?" I asked.

"It's bullshit because you know goddamn well that we're not allowing some other bitch into the equation for you to fuck, get pregnant, and fall in love with. Not happening my nigga!" Katie said seriously.

"So what do you propose?" I asked, looking from one to the other.

At first neither of them replied, but instead looked at each other for what seemed like an eternity before turning their eyes back on me.

"You do know that we're crazy right?" Honey asked.

"Of course I know that, why do you think I ever got involved with either of you."

"I suggest you don't ever forget that," Katie said.

"Trust me, I won't," I replied, laughing softly.

"Good...now get your ass in the bed, and take care of us because we're too injured to service you tonight," Honey said.

I knew that I was looking at them like I was crazy, but I had to pause and make sure that I wasn't hearing what I wanted to hear in this moment.

"I know that you heard her fool. Now bring that dick here...it's ours now."

The End

Submission Guideline

Submit the first three chapters of your completed manuscript to ldpsubmissions@gmail.com, subject line: Your book's title. The manuscript must be in a .doc file and sent as an attachment. Document should be in Times New Roman, double spaced and in size 12 font. Also, provide your synopsis and full contact information. If sending multiple submissions, they must each be in a separate email.

Have a story but no way to send it electronically? You can still submit to LDP/Ca$h Presents. Send in the first three chapters, written or typed, of your completed manuscript to:

LDP: Submissions Dept
Po Box 870494
Mesquite, Tx 75187

DO NOT send original manuscript. Must be a duplicate.

Provide your synopsis and a cover letter containing your full contact information.

Thanks for considering LDP and Ca$h Presents.

BAE BELONGS TO ME III
By **Aryanna**
THE COST OF LOYALTY **III**
By **Kweli**
CHAINED TO THE STREETS II
By **J-Blunt**
KING OF NEW YORK V
COKE KINGS IV
BORN HEARTLESS IV
By **T.J. Edwards**
GORILLAZ IN THE BAY V
TEARS OF A GANGSTA II
De'Kari
THE STREETS ARE CALLING II
Duquie Wilson
KINGPIN KILLAZ IV
STREET KINGS III
PAID IN BLOOD III
CARTEL KILLAZ IV
Hood Rich
SINS OF A HUSTLA II
ASAD
TRIGGADALE III
Elijah R. Freeman
KINGZ OF THE GAME V
Playa Ray
SLAUGHTER GANG IV

RUTHLESS HEART III
By Willie Slaughter
THE HEART OF A SAVAGE II
By Jibril Williams
FUK SHYT II
By Blakk Diamond
THE DOPEMAN'S BODYGAURD II
By Tranay Adams
TRAP GOD II
By Troublesome
YAYO III
A SHOOTER'S AMBITION II
By S. Allen
GHOST MOB
Stilloan Robinson
KINGPIN DREAMS II
By Paper Boi Rari
CREAM
By Yolanda Moore
SON OF A DOPE FIEND II
By Renta
FOREVER GANGSTA II
By Adrian Dulan
LOYALTY AIN'T PROMISED II
By Keith Williams
THE PRICE YOU PAY FOR LOVE II
By Destiny Skai

THE LIFE OF A HOOD STAR

By Rashia Wilson

TOE TAGZ III

By Ah'Million

CONFESSIONS OF A GANGSTA II

By Nicholas Lock

PAID IN KARMA II

By **Meesha**

I'M NOTHING WITHOUT HIS LOVE II

By Monet Dragun

CAUGHT UP IN THE LIFE II

By Robert Baptiste

NEW TO THE GAME II

By **Malik D. Rice**

Life of a Savage II

By **Romell Tukes**

Quiet Money II

By **Trai'Quan**

Available Now

RESTRAINING ORDER **I & II**

By **CA$H & Coffee**

LOVE KNOWS NO BOUNDARIES **I II & III**

By **Coffee**

RAISED AS A GOON I, II, III & IV

BRED BY THE SLUMS I, II, III

BLAST FOR ME I & II

ROTTEN TO THE CORE I II III

A BRONX TALE I, II, III

DUFFEL BAG CARTEL I II III IV

HEARTLESS GOON I II III IV

A SAVAGE DOPEBOY I II

HEARTLESS GOON I II III

DRUG LORDS I II III

CUTTHROAT MAFIA

By **Ghost**

LAY IT DOWN **I & II**

LAST OF A DYING BREED

BLOOD STAINS OF A SHOTTA I & II III

By **Jamaica**

LOYAL TO THE GAME I II III

LIFE OF SIN I, II III

By **TJ & Jelissa**

BLOODY COMMAS I & II

SKI MASK CARTEL I II & III

KING OF NEW YORK I II,III IV

RISE TO POWER I II III

COKE KINGS I II III

BORN HEARTLESS I II III

By **T.J. Edwards**

IF LOVING HIM IS WRONG...I & II

LOVE ME EVEN WHEN IT HURTS I II III

By **Jelissa**

WHEN THE STREETS CLAP BACK I & II III

By **Jibril Williams**

A DISTINGUISHED THUG STOLE MY HEART I II & III

LOVE SHOULDN'T HURT I II III IV

RENEGADE BOYS I II III IV

PAID IN KARMA

By **Meesha**

A GANGSTER'S CODE I &, II III

A GANGSTER'S SYN I II III

THE SAVAGE LIFE I II III

CHAINED TO THE STREETS

By J-Blunt

PUSH IT TO THE LIMIT

By **Bre' Hayes**

BLOOD OF A BOSS **I, II, III, IV, V**

SHADOWS OF THE GAME

By **Askari**

THE STREETS BLEED MURDER **I, II & III**

THE HEART OF A GANGSTA I II& III

By **Jerry Jackson**

CUM FOR ME I II III IV V

An **LDP Erotica Collaboration**

BRIDE OF A HUSTLA **I II & II**

THE FETTI GIRLS **I, II& III**

CORRUPTED BY A GANGSTA I, II III, IV

BLINDED BY HIS LOVE

THE PRICE YOU PAY FOR LOVE

By **Destiny Skai**

WHEN A GOOD GIRL GOES BAD

By **Adrienne**

THE COST OF LOYALTY I II

By Kweli

A GANGSTER'S REVENGE **I II III & IV**

THE BOSS MAN'S DAUGHTERS I II III IV V

A SAVAGE LOVE **I & II**

BAE BELONGS TO ME I II

A HUSTLER'S DECEIT I, II, III

WHAT BAD BITCHES DO I, II, III

SOUL OF A MONSTER I II III

KILL ZONE

By **Aryanna**

A KINGPIN'S AMBITON

A KINGPIN'S AMBITION **II**

I MURDER FOR THE DOUGH

By **Ambitious**

TRUE SAVAGE I II III IV V VI

DOPE BOY MAGIC I, II

MIDNIGHT CARTEL I II

By **Chris Green**

A DOPEBOY'S PRAYER

By **Eddie "Wolf" Lee**

THE KING CARTEL **I, II & III**

By **Frank Gresham**

THESE NIGGAS AIN'T LOYAL **I, II & III**

By **Nikki Tee**

GANGSTA SHYT **I II &III**

By **CATO**

THE ULTIMATE BETRAYAL

By **Phoenix**

BOSS'N UP **I , II & III**

By **Royal Nicole**

I LOVE YOU TO DEATH

By Destiny J

I RIDE FOR MY HITTA

I STILL RIDE FOR MY HITTA

By **Misty Holt**

LOVE & CHASIN' PAPER

By **Qay Crockett**

TO DIE IN VAIN

SINS OF A HUSTLA

By **ASAD**

BROOKLYN HUSTLAZ

By **Boogsy Morina**

BROOKLYN ON LOCK I & II

By **Sonovia**

GANGSTA CITY

By **Teddy Duke**

A DRUG KING AND HIS DIAMOND I & II III

A DOPEMAN'S RICHES

HER MAN, MINE'S TOO I, II

CASH MONEY HO'S

By Nicole Goosby

TRAPHOUSE KING **I II & III**

KINGPIN KILLAZ I II III

STREET KINGS I II

PAID IN BLOOD **I II**

CARTEL KILLAZ I II III

By **Hood Rich**

LIPSTICK KILLAH **I, II, III**

CRIME OF PASSION I II & III

By **Mimi**

STEADY MOBBN' **I, II, III**

THE STREETS STAINED MY SOUL

By **Marcellus Allen**

WHO SHOT YA **I, II, III**

SON OF A DOPE FIEND

Renta

GORILLAZ IN THE BAY **I II III IV**

TEARS OF A GANGSTA

DE'KARI

TRIGGADALE I II

Elijah R. Freeman

GOD BLESS THE TRAPPERS I, II, III

THESE SCANDALOUS STREETS I, II, III

FEAR MY GANGSTA I, II, III

THESE STREETS DON'T LOVE NOBODY I, II

BURY ME A G I, II, III, IV, V

A GANGSTA'S EMPIRE I, II, III, IV

THE DOPEMAN'S BODYGAURD

Tranay Adams

THE STREETS ARE CALLING

Duquie Wilson

MARRIED TO A BOSS… I II III

By Destiny Skai & Chris Green

KINGZ OF THE GAME I II III IV

Playa Ray

SLAUGHTER GANG I II III

RUTHLESS HEART I II

By Willie Slaughter

THE HEART OF A SAVAGE

By Jibril Williams

FUK SHYT

By Blakk Diamond

DON'T F#CK WITH MY HEART I II

By Linnea

ADDICTED TO THE DRAMA I II III

By Jamila

YAYO I II

A SHOOTER'S AMBITION

By S. Allen

TRAP GOD

By Troublesome

FOREVER GANGSTA

By Adrian Dulan

TOE TAGZ I II

By Ah'Million

KINGPIN DREAMS

By Paper Boi Rari

CONFESSIONS OF A GANGSTA

By Nicholas Lock

I'M NOTHING WITHOUT HIS LOVE

By Monet Dragun

CAUGHT UP IN THE LIFE

By Robert Baptiste

NEW TO THE GAME

By **Malik D. Rice**

Life of a Savage

By **Romell Tukes**

LOYALTY AIN'T PROMISED

By Keith Williams

Quiet Money

By **Trai'Quan**

BOOKS BY LDP'S CEO, CA$H

TRUST IN NO MAN

TRUST IN NO MAN 2

TRUST IN NO MAN 3

BONDED BY BLOOD

SHORTY GOT A THUG

THUGS CRY

THUGS CRY 2

THUGS CRY 3

TRUST NO BITCH

TRUST NO BITCH 2

TRUST NO BITCH 3

TIL MY CASKET DROPS

RESTRAINING ORDER

RESTRAINING ORDER 2

IN LOVE WITH A CONVICT

Coming Soon

BONDED BY BLOOD 2

BOW DOWN TO MY GANGSTA

www.ingramcontent.com/pod-product-compliance
Lightning Source LLC
Chambersburg PA
CBHW070507260626
47161CB00004B/1482